WILDER AT LAST

A STEAMY SMALL TOWN ROMANTIC COMEDY

WILDER ADVENTURES
BOOK 5

SERENA BELL

Jelsba Media Group

ISBN 978-1-953498-24-3

Mushroom icon created by Freepik from www.flaticon.com

1

HANNA

I stand back and survey my handiwork.

I'm very pleased with myself. I've covered every inch of Easton Wilder's work cube with sticky notes. His computer, his keyboard, his desk, the walls of the cube, the front of the desk. I used six different colors, arranged in many patterns, including a smiley face of sticky notes glommed on Easton's computer screen. It's basically art.

Today is Easton's birthday, and my sticky-note "gift" is payback for his last birthday "present" to me, which was replacing the contents of my deep bottom file drawer with a terrarium. Stones, little plastic plants, a leopard gecko.

Some people might call our pranks mean, but Easton and I, we've always been like this. Finding ways to make each other's lives... more colorful. More interesting. And yeah, sometimes a little more difficult—but in the best possible way.

I do a happy jiggle to celebrate my own brilliance. Easton's gonna love it. Or hate it, which is the same thing when it comes to lifetime frenemies.

On the other side of the large, converted barn that houses our offices, the door squeaks open, and I freeze.

"You must be Bear," my birthday victim says. "I'm Easton."

Oh! I forgot. It's not just Easton's birthday but also Bear Warden's first day of work. Bear is the celebrity chef that my employer, Wilder Adventures, hired to teach our clients to forage for food and then cook it in the woods over an open flame, just like Bear does on his wildly successful YouTube channel.

"Ah, right, you're the water guy," a deep, rumbly voice—exactly the kind you'd expect to hear from a man whose nickname is "Bear"—interjects.

"That's right—rafting, kayaking, and canoeing. That's me."

There's a moment of silence. I picture the two mountain men clasping and shaking big meaty paws.

Apparently, they haven't seen me yet, which makes sense, because I left the lights and heat off when I came in, in hopes of carrying out my mission undetected.

"Hey," Easton says. "We're all super glad to have you here this spring."

"Feeling's mutual," Bear replies. "It's an I-scratch-your-back-you-scratch-mine situation. My viewers are going to really dig meeting five new mountain man brothers."

"That's good news. We're planning on all this generating an insane number of new trip signups, and that's above and beyond the campers you bring in for your workshops." Easton clears his throat. "Hey, Bear?"

He sounds nervous and a little confessional. Now would be the right moment for me to unfreeze, duck out from behind this cube wall, and say hi, but Easton's tone stops me. I can't remember the last time he sounded uncertain about anything.

"Yeah?" Bear responds.

"Rumor has it you're in the market for a partner, and that you're willing to consider someone working remotely."

Wait, *what*?

"Rumor's right," Bear rumbles.

"I'd love to be on your radar screen for that."

Whoa.

Whoa!

Easton—Easton Wilder, baby brother of the Wilder family, loyal member of the Wilder Adventures business—is chasing a job *outside of Wilder*.

Leaving Wilder.

My hands are cold. Probably because I never turned on the lights or the heat. Definitely because of that. It's barely sixty degrees in here.

"Absolutely," Bear responds. "I don't have anyone yet that I'm all-in on, so I'd be happy to consider you. I like what you're doing with the Wilder TikTok and YouTube—those are new, right?"

"Yeah. Insta didn't feel like enough for what we were trying to do."

"No, no, it's not—your instincts are dead on," Bear says heartily. "I'll take a closer look, but I liked what I saw. You know your brother is assigning two of his people to be co-leaders with me, right?"

"That's why I'm bringing this up now. I'd like to be one of them."

Oh. No. Apart from the deep weirdness of learning that

Easton might be quitting the family business, it's inconvenient that he wants to be a co-leader on Bear's trip, because I also wanted to be one of them. Easton and I don't get assigned to stuff together. Gabe—our boss and Easton's oldest brother—will basically do anything to avoid having us work together. Something about *squabbling like four-year-olds*.

He's not wrong.

Easton continues, "If you liked what you saw on TikTok and YouTube, and you could mention that to Gabe, it'll give him a prod to make me one of the co-leaders."

"I can do that," Bear says.

I can't stand here any longer, hiding in plain sight. I have to turn around and reveal to Easton that I've overheard his whole conversation and know he's thinking about bailing out of Wilder Adventures.

For one thing, it's wrong to eavesdrop.

For another, I can't pass up an opportunity to make Easton squirm.

I turn and step out of his cube, intending to say, "Easton Wilder, wait till your big brother hears about this!"

Of course, I won't actually tell Gabe. I give Easton shit for sport, but that doesn't mean I want him to get taken apart molecule by molecule by his boss and sibling.

But whatever I was planning or not planning to say, it's moot. The words dry up on my tongue.

Bear Warden on the screen did *not* prepare me for Bear Warden in the flesh. He's gorgeous.

I mean, not quite as gorgeous as Easton, standing beside him, but ever since Easton started dating mean girls in middle school, I've discounted him as a *man* and thought of him more as a work of art with a sense of humor and bad taste in women. It's a helpful, ever-present reminder that he's off limits, even as an object of fantasy.

The man next to Easton is probably six-foot-four. Broad as a barn, though not the Wilder-brother molded-from-marble version. Softer, more dad-bodied—if your dad was a grizzly bear. He has reddish-brown hair, a thick and impeccably trimmed coppery beard, full lips, and bright blue eyes. Up close, he's vivid.

Something has happened to my brain.

Well, really, to my body.

As in, my body—specifically, my vagina—hijacked all the blood from my brain.

Which is a big deal, because ever since I moved Easton from the middle-school-crush category to *nope*, this doesn't happen to me very often, with men or women.

When I recover the power of speech, I've completely borked my stick-it-to-Easton entrance, and all I can say is, "Hey. I'm Hanna Hott." And I extend my hand.

"Very nice to meet you, Hanna," Bear says, taking my hand in his. His dwarfs mine—and I'm used to outsized men. "It's always a delight to meet women who love the woods."

I leave my hand where it is a beat too long, enjoying the giantness of his, and the warmth, and the way his eyes are locked onto mine. I'm not sure anyone has ever delivered quite so much eye contact over a handshake. I'm a fan.

"I'm yours," I blurt. Then I hear myself, clap a hand over my mouth, and correct, "I mean, I'm a huge *fan* of yours!"

Bear beams. "I'm flattered," he says, all grizzly gruff. I

swear I can feel the bass tones of his voice in my underpants. That's a thing, right?

I'm not sure what to say next, because there are no words in my brain.

"Bear," Easton says. "You'll have to excuse us for a moment. Hanna and I have to settle a quick work-related issue before the team meeting starts." And he grabs my arm and hustles me toward the front of the converted barn that houses the Wilder offices.

My eyes, still on Bear, are quite likely the last part of me to leave headquarters before Easton yanks me out of the big red barn and into the watery Oregon spring sunshine. The air's still morning-moist, the summer dust not yet kicked up, the smell of juniper and sage rich in my nose. We're standing on former ranch land, nestled in a stand of windbreak trees that surround the original house and barn.

"Hanna," Easton demands. "What did you hear. I'm sorry. Overhear?"

"*Everything.*"

His eyes get even bigger. I've known Easton since we started kindergarten in the same classroom, and it's not easy to throw him off his game. I think that's part of what's so fun about giving him a hard time; it's like hitting a Weeble. It wobbles, but it always bounces back.

Even in this case. It takes him a beat longer than usual, but he finds his feet. I can tell because he shutters the panic behind his eyes and gives me a classic Easton smirk.

"But I know you won't tell Gabe," he says. "Because this is your perfect opportunity to get rid of me. If I'm working remotely for Bear, I won't be around Wilder headquarters nearly as much." He gestures to the barn. "And wouldn't that be your dream?" He's teasing, eyebrow raised. "Just think of how much more peaceful your life would be."

Okay. Maybe. But I have questions. So many questions. Why does he want the Bear job? Does he think he'll get it?

And why am I not jumping for joy at the news that Easton might not be around Wilder headquarters quite as often?

Although I know the answer to that question. Because as much hell as Easton and I give each other, at bottom, he's probably the biggest certainty of my life, after death and taxes. And the idea of him leaving Wilder doesn't sit nicely in the pit of my stomach.

That said, no way I'm going to tell him.

"It *is* my dream," I say. "This is like Christmas and Halloween and my birthday all in one. What can I do to help you get the job?"

"Well, first off, don't tell Gabe," he says, tipping his head toward the ranch house on the other side of the headquarters parking lot, where his brother's family lives. "And do whatever you can to help me convince Gabe I should be one of the two co-leaders."

I frown. "About that. I don't think that's in my best interest."

Easton scowls. "What do you mean, not in your best interest?"

"I mean, *I* want to be one of the co-leaders. And Gabe's never going to put both of us on the same trip, because— well, you know how he feels about what happened last time."

"Why do you want to be a co-leader?" Easton demands. "Is it just to mess with my plans?"

"Hey! Do you really think I'm that vicious?" I hold up a hand. "Never mind, don't answer that. This has nothing to do with you, you egotist. It's because Gabe is phasing out winter trips."

"What? I know he was getting rid of skiing, but not winter trips in general."

"Yeah, well, none of the stuff we put in place to replace it has been a winner. And with my business unit partner *finding himself* with his whole photography thing…"

A pained expression crosses Easton's face at this characterization of his brother Kane, but he just nods.

"…basically, I need to carve out a new niche for myself. My plan is to learn as much as I can from Bear this spring. Then I'll add foraging and cooking to the glamping and Gilderness trips."

Easton squints. "So… what you're saying is… we both want to be a co-leader, and there's no way Gabe's going to let us do it together, so it's… what, a fight to the death?"

"Basically."

He crosses his arms. "You can't just let me have it because it's important to me?"

"I could ask you the same question," I point out.

The corners of his mouth turn up, but he flattens his lips so I won't see him smiling. I savor his struggle.

"Yup," I say. "Fight to the death."

He shakes his head in disgust, but he's still trying not to smile.

2

EASTON

Before Hanna and I can head back inside, Gabe and his wife Lucy appear on the broad front porch of their house, descend the steps, and stroll our way.

At the same time, two cars—one with my brother Brody and my mom, and the other with my brothers Clark and Kane, pull into the gravel lot.

It's a Wilder quorum.

In the Wilder way, everyone greets one another with big hugs, like it's been weeks since we've gathered, instead of less than twenty-four hours.

"Bear's inside," I inform them, pointing to the barn that houses headquarters. Both the barn and Gabe's house used to be part of the old ranch; my granddad sold off the land to build this business. Now, through a series of twists and turns, my brothers and I own most of it—and run it.

"What are you two doing out here?" Gabe—aka the boss—demands. "You should be inside treating him like royalty. Please don't tell me you were squabbling in front of him."

"No!" we both say at exactly the same time, and too vehemently.

He looks from me to Hanna and back again, eyes narrow.

"Swear," Hanna says, crossing her heart.

"I better not hear otherwise," Gabe mutters.

We all head inside, where Gabe greets Bear with what I know from experience is a bone-crunching handshake and introduces him around.

Bear nods with each new person. "You'll have to excuse me if I get you all mixed up a few times at first," he says. "I'm not the best with names and faces."

"No worries," Gabe says. "We're a lot."

"I've got Barb, Lucy, and Hanna down." Bear smiles at each as he names them. He turns to Hanna last, and his smile lingers on her.

Hanna blushes.

Wait. A. Second.

No, I didn't imagine it. Yes, her cheeks are definitely pink. Even after Bear turns his gaze back to the rest of us, surveying the Wilder-brother landscape with understandable confusion, her eyes stay on his face.

Hanna has a crush.

Hanna has a *crush*.

I think back to earlier. If I hadn't been so torqued over the fact that Hanna overheard my conversation with Bear, I would have paid more attention to her behavior. And then I would have registered the fact that it was tremendously un-Hanna-like to say, "I'm a huge fan of yours."

It's un-Hanna-like to have a crush at all. In all the time I've known her, she never has, or at least not that I've been aware of. I know she's gone on a few dates this year, but I've never gotten the impression that any of those men or women have registered on her Richter scale of hopefuls.

Truth is, I've always wondered what it would take to bring Hanna Hott to her knees.

Apparently, all it takes is a celebrity chef-slash-forager with a thick and expensively barbered beard and clothes that are meant to look like "I stumbled out of a tent in what I wore yesterday" but probably cost a thousand dollars.

Also, for years I've coveted the hiking boots he's wearing. I know they ring in at five hundred.

I feel a stab of irritation toward Bear, which makes zero sense, because *of course* a famous YouTuber and influencer would put a lot of effort into his appearance.

And if I get the job with Bear, I'll be doing the same thing. Five-hundred-dollar hiking boots, here I come.

Bear delivers a spiel about himself. He was a chef first, then discovered foraging and started vlogging about it. Before long, he'd turned it into a whole survivalist-chef schtick on YouTube, and after he spent three months in the woods, living off gourmet meals, his channel went viral.

"I'm going to run these trips just like what you see on my show. Hike in, forage for what's in season—berries, ferns, nettles, miner's lettuce, you know the deal. We do a bit of fishing with homemade rods and snaring with homemade traps. Then we cook it up over an open flame. We won't know in advance what we're going to find or what we're going to be eating—that's the most exciting part."

He scans the table. "Clark, right?" He makes eye contact with my middle brother. "This is your thing, isn't it?"

"Not the way you do it," Clark says. "Not where it's a gourmet feast."

Bear grins, a flash of white teeth. It's clear why this guy's show took off. He's charismatic. Dynamic. "That's the part I love. It's a lot of improv, a lot of brainstorming, a lot of taking input from the participants. I enlist everyone's help —gathering, collecting, coming up with recipes. People get into it, *really* into it, and that part's a thrill, too."

I catch another round of admiring glances from the women at the table. Including Hanna, whose mouth is open. Lush lower lip sagging in awe and, I'd wager, lust.

Gabe nods. "You tell us what you need, we'll make sure you have it."

Bear's gaze circles our group. "I'd appreciate a couple of co-leaders, like we talked about. Frees me up to focus on filming and the workshop—"

"I want to do it," Hanna says.

The fact that Hanna doesn't give a shit about the normal rules of engagement gives her an unfair advantage in fights to the death.

"Hanna would be a great choice," Bear says, giving her another warm smile. She pinks up again. Hanna has very light skin and very dark hair, and when she sunburns or blushes, it's obvious. And pretty, all roses-and-cream. Like a round-cheeked Snow White.

I frown at myself for this weird flight of fancy.

Bear is still eyeing Hanna appraisingly. "My viewers would love seeing you on camera."

Her blush deepens.

"A woman kicking ass in the woods is a selling point," he goes on.

Hanna's shoulders slump, just a degree—pretty sure no one but me even noticed. I'm simultaneously annoyed at Bear for leading her on with that first flirty sentence and at Hanna for letting herself be led.

When Hanna is brought to her knees, she apparently goes hard.

But I won't let my sympathy for Hanna weaken my position in this fight. Ever since Kane shared his revelation last year that what he really wants to do is photography, I've been wrestling with wanting to find my own path, too, outside the Wilder Adventures world. As the youngest Wilder, and the perennial class clown, I always struggle. I'm pretty sure that as long as I'm Baby Wilder, I'll never be taken seriously. Hence wanting to find a whole new direction for myself in the Bear Warden empire.

"I'd like to be one of the co-leaders," I chime in. "I bet my TikTok and YouTube experience would be a big asset." I launch a triumphant glance across the table at Hanna, who rolls her eyes.

Gabe's eyebrows go up as he looks from Hanna to me. "You both want to do this. The two of you." It's not a question. It's an expression of apprehension and disbelief.

Just like Hanna said, Gabe will *not* want to put the two of us on a trip together.

Bear nods my way. "I've seen Easton's TikToks and YouTubes. He's got a strong presence on video." He looks from me to Hanna. "And I love your enthusiasm, both of you." He turns to Gabe next. "If you can spare these two, I'd love to work with them."

Hanna and I exchange startled glances. It hadn't

occurred to either of us that Bear would go to bat for both of us as a team and make it difficult for Gabe to refuse him.

If Gabe can't refuse Bear and lets us work together... we'll both get what we want.

But also, we'll be stuck in the woods together while I try to get a job from Bear, and she tries to... get... whatever it is she wants from him.

Hanna, who has presumably reached the same conclusion, looks as alarmed as I feel.

For once, we're in agreement.

As soon as the meeting breaks up, I head back to my cube. Hanna trails me.

"Why are you following me?"

"No reason," she says, shrugging.

"Well, stop."

But she stays half a step behind me, and I can still feel her breathing down the back of my neck when I step into my work area and see...

Holy shit.

She has sticky-noted my entire cube. Every. Last. Square. Inch.

And there's a big box of Morning Rush Coffee and donuts on my (sticky-noted) chair.

"Happy birthday," she says, shrugging.

I'm oddly touched. First of all, Hanna is the only one so far to remember that it's my birthday, which is not an uncommon problem in a family with six kids. But also, Hanna is not an early riser, and she's not a methodical person. Not the kind of person you would imagine painstakingly sticky-noting an entire cubicle. Definitely not in the earliest hours of the day.

"You must have had to get up at, what, like, three a.m. to do this?"

"Don't get too weepy," she says. "I ate five of your donuts. I forgot breakfast."

I swallow a laugh.

Gabe sticks his head in.

"Whoa," he says, surveying my rainbow territory. And then, "Jesus. Hanna. Did you do that? That glue better not ruin any office property."

We both roll our eyes. Usually we roll them *at* each other, but Gabe has the power to make us roll them in tandem, and at him.

"Can I see both of you in my office?"

We skulk there, stealing glances at each other that say, *Do you know what this is about? Nope, me neither.*

Once we're seated across from him, Gabe cuts to the chase:

"If I let you two co-lead these Bear trips, and that's a *big* if, I better not hear that either of you, or more to the point *both of you*, have been a distraction. Like *pranks*," he says, giving Hanna the evil eye.

He doesn't know about the terrarium I installed in her file drawer on her last birthday. Her sticky notes are an excellent rejoinder.

Gabe scowls even deeper. "Or what happened on the singles trip."

"In fairness," I respond, "the campers on that trip *loved* us."

We're both referring to the singles adventure that Hanna and I led together. Everyone raved about the outing on the feedback forms—"especially the absolutely adorable squabbling married couple who led it."

Hanna and I had looked in horror at each other when we saw ourselves referred to as married.

Squabbling, we could live with.

In fairness, I can see the comparison to an old married couple. We do fight like people who've been at each other's throats for fifty years. Although I think we're more like two puppies in the same litter. We've known each other since kindergarten; we're both youngest children; and we're used to defending our tiny sliver of personal territory in big families. Plus, we're opposites in almost every way—she's grumpy and blunt and a scrappy fighter, and I'm charming and flirtatious—to a fault.

"And *you*," Gabe says, aiming a fierce glare at me, like he somehow heard my internal monologue. "You in particular need to be careful not to draw attention away from Bear. He has to be the main attraction on these trips. Got it?"

Those same feedback forms from the singles trip also featured an outraged man who wanted his money back because I'd flirted with too many women on that trip, thus depriving him of his rightful chance to—no kidding, his words, "bag a babe like I paid for."

Credit where credit is due: Gabe did call up the guy and have a serious conversation with him about his entitlement and the need to respect women, which couldn't have been fun.

But he's never quite let it go.

"That wasn't Easton's fault."

Hanna's defense startles me. I give her a questioning look, and she gives me a slight nod in return. Usually, Hanna's on the other side of this argument—trying to get me in trouble with someone or other. I guess she's decided the best way to get what *she* wants is for both of us to get what *we* want, and she might not be wrong. "He wasn't flirting. He was just being himself." She pauses and shoots me a sideways look. Uh-oh. So much for supportive. I can see mischief coming. "He can't help it if women fall out of their clothes around him."

"See, this is exactly what I'm talking about," Gabe says in exasperation. "I can't possibly send both of you on another trip together. Hanna—"

We don't get to find out what he's about to say, whether he's about to dismiss her or appoint her.

"I think it's perfect."

Lucy, Gabe's wife and the architect of Wilder Adventures' current marketing plan, stands in the doorway.

"We know from those feedback forms that campers find these two adorable. Why wouldn't Bear's guests and his YouTube audience feel the same way? I think they're perfect for the Wilder vibe."

All three of us stare at her.

"They're funny, they're fun, they're high-spirited, and they'll both look great on camera."

"You're talking about me, right?" Hanna asks Lucy. "No one has *ever* said I was photogenic."

"I beg to differ, hon," Lucy says. "With your coloring?"

Ah. So I'm not the only one who thinks Hanna looks like Snow White.

Lucy shrugs. "I mean, it's not like you have other volunteers, either. Clark and Brody are booked solid, Kane's up to his ears in photography and fatherhood—Easton, you've got a fair amount on your schedule, true, but it dovetails pretty nicely with Bear's workshop schedule. And Hanna's basically free. Unless *you're* thinking of going," she says, giving Gabe a look that very clearly suggests he'd better not be, not with a toddler at home.

Gabe might have stood a chance against the two of us, but he's hopeless when it comes to Lucy. We've all known that ever since she arrived in Rush Creek to help Wilder Adventures capitalize on our town's new wedding-and-spa tourists—and went head-to-head with him.

He throws up his hands. "Okay," he says. "I think it's a terrible idea, but if we listened to me, we'd be out of business right now. Best business decision I ever didn't make was hiring Lucy; best professional development I ever undertook was learning to listen to her." He eyes both of us. "You guys are going into the woods together. Please don't kill each other. And for pity's sake, don't make me regret this."

"We won't," Hanna and I say at the same time.

We don't look at each other. I think we both know that's a promise neither of us feels confident making.

3

———————

HANNA

"So, you grew up in these woods?"

Bear Warden's voice is deep, honey rich, and solicitous as he gestures at the dense evergreen forest around us. It's two weeks after his arrival in Rush Creek, and this is the first time he's taken a group into the woods for one of his workshops.

I hate talking about myself. At the same time, there's something absolutely amazing about being asked to. I can't remember the last time that happened. Definitely not on any of the dates I've been on this year.

"Technically…" I launch in. "I grew up on a ranch. But as soon as I was old enough, I started hiking." I pick my way over a rocky stretch of path. "And I always knew I wanted to work for Wilder Adventures."

"Really? Why?"

The trail has evened out, enough that I can meet Bear's curious gaze. He has this way of holding my eyes with his vivid blue ones that makes me feel wobbly in the midsection. Like everything I have to say is infinitely interesting to him.

"Well," I start in. "I knew I didn't ever want an office job, and that I wanted an outdoors job. And I thought what the Wilders did was the coolest thing I'd ever seen."

We have to stop where a log has fallen across the path. It's partially rotten and covered with moss. Bear reaches out a big paw to take my hand and guide me over the log. Then he hesitates.

"Hey," he says softly. "I know you're tough as nails and can take care of yourself. But—let me help you?"

Oh, wow.

"Uh, okay," I manage, taking the offered hand and letting him help me.

No Wilder brother has ever done anything like that. To be fair, I would have kicked them in the balls if they'd tried. But still.

When I was little, my mom used to call me her princess, which I *hated*. I had five older brothers, and I wanted to be just like them. But with me, my mom had finally gotten her coveted daughter, and she wanted me to be her little girl.

When I fought her about calling me her princess, she said that someday there would be a guy who treated me like one, and I wouldn't mind.

I'd told her she was wrong.

And for years, I believed it. We never figured out how to reconcile what I wanted with what she wanted; and then she was gone.

But lately? I've started to think maybe it wouldn't be the worst fate in the world.

"Chin up higher, Hanna!"

The voice belongs to Bear's assistant, Cypress, a tall, lean, long-haired whirlwind of energy who's an expert at walking backwards on uneven terrain. They take only the occasional peek over their shoulder. It's very impressive. They're filming us as we walk and talk, which is the only thing that slightly mars my mood. Bear and I each have mics clipped to our backpack straps, to capture the conversation.

We pass out of the thick trees and into a more exposed stretch of sunny trail.

"How long have you been working with Bear?" I ask Cypress.

They peek out from behind the camera, rewarding my question with a shy smile. "Two and a half years. I had my own foraging channel, but it wasn't going anywhere, and Bear reached out to me to say he loved my cinematography and would I consider working for him."

"No coincidence that I went viral for the first time six months after Cypress started." Bear drops a nod of appreciation toward his assistant. "I couldn't do my job without them. I had to beg them to come with me to Rush Creek."

I raise my eyebrows. "Oh, yeah? You didn't want to leave Golden for Rush Creek?"

"Mostly, I didn't want to abandon my garden. I'm a big gardener." Cypress beams. "And I left a bunch of seedlings in the care of my stoner roommate who sometimes doesn't remember to feed himself, let alone care for other life forms."

I have known stoners. Makes sense.

"So I make him FaceTime me every evening. Proof of life. The plants, not him. He's dispensable."

I snort-laugh.

Cypress tucks themself behind the camera again and drops back to filming distance. I get the distinct feeling it's their happy place.

"How old were you when you started working for Wilder?" Bear shifts the focus to me.

"Fourteen. I couldn't lead trips yet, but I went on them and assisted the Wilders. Learned everything they knew, or close to it, and was leading my own trips by the time I was sixteen."

"I have so much respect for that," Bear says. "I was a slow starter myself. Bummed around a bunch, then went to culinary school, then was a chef until I realized it wasn't doing it for me, then *finally* figured out I was meant to be outdoors. And *then* got started doing it on video. But you—you knew who you were from the beginning."

"Not so sure about that," I say, but my laugh doesn't quite make it out of my mouth.

It's not so much that I don't know who I am: I do. What I'm not quite so sure about is where I fit in. Sometimes I feel like I'm not entirely one of the girls and I'm not entirely one of the guys. Since my brothers left Rush Creek, there hasn't really been a Hott family to feel part of... and although the Wilders have never done anything to make me feel lesser, I'm not truly a Wilder.

This last year or so, I've started to register that maybe I'm lonely.

We stop to let the others catch up. I switch off my mic and grab a moment in the woods by myself for a bio break, then come back to find everyone picking salmon berries.

"Hold out your hand," Bear says, and drops a few ripe

ones, red as raspberries, into my palm. My chest gets warm with the pleasure of being cared for. And Cypress's not even filming us; they're focused right now on a small group of women oohing over the flavor of the berries, which, it's true, are *like the love child of a berry and rhubarb*.

I lick the last of the berry juice off my palm and look up to discover Easton watching me with a complicated expression on his face.

Cypress wants Bear to hang back a bit from the group, so when the hike starts up again, Easton falls in beside me.

"Someone's got a crush," he teases.

"I don't know what you're talking about."

"I mean, he's good," Easton says. "Have to give him credit. Helping you over the log. Feeding you berries. I'd have a crush, too."

"I don't have a crush!"

"Suuuuure you don't. That's why your face turns red every time he smiles at you."

"You're such a dick," I tell him.

"And you are so full of it. You didn't want to come on this trip because you wanted to find a new role for yourself at Wilder. You came on the trip because you wanted to get laid. And," he says, raising his eyebrows, "you appear to be on the path to success."

"Go pick on someone else." But I'm smiling at his last observation. If Easton Wilder, panty-melter extraordinaire, thinks I'm making inroads with Bear, he has to be right.

"You grew up with five mountain men up in your business 24/7—I would not have picked you to go all squishy over one. I would have pegged you to fall for a poet-professor."

"Ugh, no way. And I'm not 'all squishy.'"

"You looked pretty squishy there for a bit. Big eyes, looking through the eyelashes…" He demonstrates, ducking to blink up at me. Up close, Easton's eyes are a gorgeous shade of green, which I forget for long stretches of time. He's objectively insanely good-looking, which I also forget, because it's useless information, along the lines of, *the sky is blue,* or *the sun is a flaming ball of gas.* Something true but also so fundamental that you take it for granted.

"I was *not* squishy."

"Tell it to the jury," he says, but he's laughing, and I'm laughing, too, despite myself. There's just something about Easton; he makes everything less serious, including me. He lightens things so they make sense again.

Plus, he thinks Bear is into me…

Bear Warden is *into* me.

Despite the forty-pound weight on my back, I practically skip the next stretch of path.

LATER, we make camp near a mountain lake, so clear you can see stones on its bottom, the mountains sharp and capped with the last of the spring snow. The air is scented with Ponderosa pine and woodsmoke, two of my favorite smells. Easton and I wander through the ranks of our participants, helping them with tasks Bear has laid out—setting snares, netting fish, starting cookfires, harvesting fiddleheads and miner's lettuce, searching for trailing blackberry, Oregon grape, and candy flower.

Bear has done a good job of creating little teams and

building camaraderie among the participants, and Cypress circulates, too, capturing conversations and moments of triumph on video.

"Did you get your proof of life this morning?" I ask when they pass by. "The seedlings?"

Cypress wrinkles their nose unhappily. "He forgot to water them last night, but they hung in there."

"You might need a new roommate?" I suggest.

"I might," they agree, the corner of their mouth ticking up.

One cookfire is being particularly persnickety, so Easton calls me over—I've got some fire-whisperer genes—and the two of us fiddle with the bow until we've got a small flame. Easton grabs dry grass and bark for kindling, and I nurse the fire to a decent size.

"It's like magic," one of the women in an awestruck couple tells me.

"It's just practice," I tell her. "I've been doing it for—God, decades. Just keep after it. You'll get there."

"We're more the car-camp-once-in-a-while-for-fun types," her wife says, and they smile at each other.

"Then just let us help you, and enjoy yourselves," I tell them.

When we step away, Easton says, "I always forget."

"Forget what?"

"That you can be nice when you want to be. When it's not me."

"I'm sometimes nice to you."

"When?"

I pretend to think. "There was that time back in... okay, no. That was someone else."

Easton rolls his eyes at me.

A movement across the clearing catches my eye. It's Bear, bending to squat beside another cookfire, one tended by a pretty redhead wearing a flattering fleece top and my favorite brand of hiking pants. Bear's head is inclined toward hers, and I can hear enough of the cadence of their conversation to tell he's asking her questions as he puts his hands over hers and guides the movement of the fire bow. And she looks up at him through her eyelashes, smitten and confiding.

Something dark caves in midway through my chest.

I sneak a look at Easton. He's watching Bear, too, and scowling. Then he shifts his attention to me, and his expression softens at whatever he sees on my face. Damn it, he'd better not be feeling sorry for me.

He opens his mouth as if to say something, takes another long look at me, and seems to think better of it. He turns away for a moment. When he turns back, the expression on his face is altogether different, teasing and wry.

"Good thing you don't have a crush on him." The corner of his mouth turns up.

He takes a few steps, bends down, and picks up a stone, holding it out to me.

THE FIRST TIME Easton ever did that was at my mom's funeral. We were nine, and our early-elementary school chumminess had given way to blood-sport—keep-away games at recess, girls against boys. I loved those games, and the trash talk that went with them. It was way easier for a boy and girl to be frenemies than friends.

After the service, when people were eating and talking, I couldn't stay in the funeral home. I hated the way it smelled—cloyingly of flowers—but mostly I hated how everyone kept trying to talk to me about how I felt.

I left and wandered down to the river where I stood looking out at the water, trying not to cry. None of my brothers had cried, and I sure didn't want to. It felt like I'd be betraying the sisterhood if the only girl was the first sibling to go to pieces.

Someone stepped up beside me and slid something cool and hard into my hand. Heavy and smooth and flat. A skipping stone. I chucked it across the water, watching it bounce off the gleaming surface. The act of doing that, of doing *something*, cleared out some of the pressure in my chest.

The person beside me held out another stone. I turned, and it was Easton. He didn't say anything, and neither did I, but I remembered that he'd lost his dad less than two years earlier.

So he knew.

I took the stone from him and skipped it. It bounced one, two, three, four, five times off the water and sank.

He handed me stones, one by one, both of us utterly silent, until dark fell and my granddad sent my brothers to find me and take me home.

Easton and I have never mentioned that day, not once, since.

I don't mention it now. I just say, "Yeah. Good thing I don't have a crush on him," and take the stone.

I slide it into my pocket, where it clicks against the one that's in there now. I think that's the one he gave me the day Gabe told me Wilder was phasing out ski trips.

Bear murmurs one last thing to the woman he's been helping, rises to his feet, claps his hands to get our attention, and announces that it's time to start cooking.

He does his food magic, farming out bits of the cooking to each of the fires he's ordered into existence, demonstrating how to use a minimal number of tools to turn our foraged treasures into something gourmet. The starter is nettle soup. The entree is lake trout with berry coulis—which is just *sauce*, but the sponsors who pay Bear millions per year to wear their clothes and boots and use their camping and cooking equipment want him to say something fancier than "sauce." The side dish features fiddlehead ferns in a chicory-pine nut pesto.

"Hey," Easton says, appearing beside me. "I can't finish my trout—you want the rest of it?"

"Hell yes," I say, and he scrapes his portion onto my plate. "Just don't think I'm going to trade you anything for it."

Easton holds up two hands, laughing. "I know you don't share your food."

I point my camping fork at him. "Damn straight."

"Here," he says, pointing at my empty soup bowl. "Give me that; I'll wash it."

I gratefully turn it over to him, and he takes it to the camp "sink."

When we're done with dinner, Bear serves dessert. I'm disappointed he cheated on the pièce de résistance, foraged berry cobbler. He packed in the ingredients to make the dough. But my disappointment vaporizes when Bear plops down beside me as I glide the first spoonful into my mouth.

"Oh, my God," I moan.

Bear beams. "There's nothing better than a woman who knows how to appreciate food," he murmurs.

"There's nothing better than a man who cooks," I fire back.

Bear's eyes find mine, full of appreciation. "I'm sorry the evening got away from me," he says. "There are always so many people needing my time and help, and I can't always give it to the people I most want to." He holds my gaze, and I feel like the boundary lines of my body are dissolving under his regard.

Cypress appears at Bear's shoulder. "Bear, I'm sorry to interrupt, but there's a raccoon hanging around the food, and I need you to do an episode of Bear versus The Raccoon."

"Bear versus The Raccoon?" I manage, with something like a straight face.

Bear gives me an apologetic smile. "I'm sorry," he says, touching my hand. "We've got this ongoing schtick where I do mock battle with a raccoon. Always on for the camera, you know? I'll catch up with you later. Just know I'd rather be chatting with you."

I watch him go, unable to take my eyes off his ass in his hiking pants, which look like they were tailored onto his body.

I stay there for a long time, feeling resentful of an innocent trash panda, hoping Bear will reappear. The fire I'm closest to starts to die down to coals, and the cold of the woods creeps into my bones.

"Hey," Easton says from behind me.

"Hey," I say back.

"You should go to bed."

"In a little," I say.

He raises an eyebrow. "Okay, then," he says. "I'm turning in. Don't do anything I wouldn't do with our trip leader."

"Pretty sure that doesn't rule anything out, Mr. Easy."

"*With our trip leader*," he repeats, laughing, walking backwards away from me.

I roll my eyes and bite back my smile.

4

—————

EASTON

"If I admit I have a crush, will you help me?"

Hanna stands in front of me inside Wilder headquarters a few days after the first Bear trip, arms crossed over one of her ubiquitous baggy sweatshirts. That woman has more baggy sweatshirts than a Walmart.

We're the last two people left at headquarters tonight. I don't know what she's still doing here, but I'm finishing up some paperwork for Bear's trip. Celebrities don't have to do their own paperwork.

"What are you talking about?" I ask.

"If I admit I have a crush on Bear Warden, will you help me get the guy?"

"I'm going to pinch myself right now, because if you're asking me for help, I'm definitely dreaming."

"You're not dreaming," she informs me. "But if you want me to pinch you—"

"Not necessary!" I say, jumping out of her reach. "But I would like you to say the humiliating part again. About how you have a terrible, mad, soul-wrenching crush—"

"I didn't say any of that."

"And only I, Easton Wilder, can help you win him over and live happily ever after."

"Fine," she says. "I have a terrible, mad, soul-wrenching crush, and only you, Easton Panty-Melter Wilder, have the expertise in lurrrrrvvvving to help me find my way to bliss."

"That wasn't quite as satisfying as I'd hoped," I admit. In fact, the word *bliss* in conjunction with Bear makes me strangely itchy.

"Seriously, Easton, help me."

"Help you what?"

"Woo Bear. Get laid."

"That's it? That's your highest aspiration? From the way you were looking at him, I thought it was going to be more like a white wedding and four-point-five kids."

"Why are kids always measured in halves? It's so awful to contemplate. Which half would you get?"

"You're deflecting."

"True," she admits.

"You want more than just to have sex with him."

She scrunches up her whole face—oddly cute—and then relaxes it. "Look," she says, pointing a finger at me. "I think you know I've been on a few dates this year."

"Rumor had reached me, yes."

"And that means you probably know that they haven't been a rip-roaring success."

In the interest of honesty, I say, "Um. Yeah."

"Not to get into the nitty-gritty details, but they basically break down into two categories. People who are secretly married, and people who are totally and completely unacceptable for coffee and a sticky bun, let along marriage and procreation."

"That sounds—unfun."

"So. Un. Fun."

"I'm sorry."

"Here's the thing. I *like* Bear. I like him a lot. He's…"

She hesitates, and I'm a hundred percent sure I don't want her to finish the sentence, although I'm not sure how I know.

"…really fucking hot."

Yeah, didn't need that sentence finished.

"But that's not the main thing. The main thing is, he has a great job and a serious career, he loves the outdoors, and he's got ambitions. And he knows how to treat a woman. He's the whole package. And I've seen enough this year to know that when a guy who's the whole package comes along, you don't hang back and 'see what happens next.' You go for it."

I'm not nearly as pleased about getting her to agree that she wants Bear for more than sex as I was expecting to be. In fact, I wish she'd stuck to her guns and insisted this was just an itch to be scratched.

Although, either way, it's a terrible idea. I don't think Bear is a bad person; I just think he's a bit of an egotist. A camera ham. And Hanna deserves better than a man who's treating her well for the sake of looking good to his audience and sponsors. And who's also treating other women well at the same time, for the same reasons.

That said, I want her to be happy, especially if I quit working for Wilder and can't look out for her on a daily basis.

Hanna would disembowel me with a blunt pencil if she knew I "looked out for her" but it's true. I do. And fixing her up with Bear really doesn't fit my idea of what it means to keep an eye on her well-being.

"What do you want me to do, exactly?" I ask, in lieu of explaining how I feel about her well-being, which will make Hanna squirmy. Hanna hates feelings—everyone else's, definitely, but even more so, her own. "Are we talking, like, a makeover montage situation? Where you suddenly have long hair and lots of makeup and an evening gown, and he can't stop staring at you from across the room?"

"I can't suddenly have long hair," Hanna points out. "I mean, unless I wear a wig, but that seems like it would have unintended consequences in a dating scenario."

"You know what I mean. Changing yourself for a guy is a bad idea. Any guy who needs you to look different from how you look now doesn't deserve you."

"When I was little," Hanna says, "my mom used to try to get me to wear dresses."

This is intriguing. Hanna *never* talks about her mom. In fact, I literally don't think she has mentioned her mother to me once since her death. So, for once, I don't make a snide comment about what a low probability of success trying to get Hanna to wear a dress must have had.

Her eyes are a little dreamy, as if she's remembering. "I would yell at her that anyone who didn't like me the way I was didn't deserve to see me at their party-slash-concert-slash-whatever. And she'd respond, *It's a costume, baby. It's armor. It's plumage. It doesn't change who you are, it just lets you walk into battle your strongest self.*"

I know better than to say anything. Hanna talks like this so infrequently that when it happens, I know just to listen.

"This is like that. I just want to gird myself. Fluff my feathers. Swirl my cape." She sighs. "I want to get his undivided, off-camera attention—is that so wrong?"

It's the sigh that gets to me. More than anything else in the world, I hate seeing Hanna defeated. All I can manage is, "No. But maybe I'm not the guy for this job, Han. What about your girls? They'd be all over this. They'd have you decked out for battle in a second."

"No," she says decisively. "No women. They'll want to talk about feelings. They'll want to analyze everything and scrutinize my facial expressions, and I'll end up confessing I masturbate thinking about him."

My mouth falls open. This is not a sentence I expected to come out of Hanna's mouth, and I'll admit, it catches me off guard. In the "it's weird when your friend talks dirty unexpectedly" way. Like suddenly I'm thinking about Hanna, masturbating, which is, oddly, not a bad thought at all, although Hanna masturbating thinking about Bear Warden...

I don't like that nearly as much.

But I digress.

"I don't know, Han. I think me coaching you on how to get a guy? It's a bad idea. On all fronts."

"Yeah," she says. "I thought you might say that. So... here's the thing, Easton. I really didn't want to have to do this, but..."

No good ever came of a sentence that started like that.

"...if you don't want me to tell Gabe that you're trying to get a job with Bear, you have to help me."

She went there. She really went there.

"You'd do that? Betray me?"

"I'd so much rather not." Her voice is apologetic.

I don't have to think about it very long. How angry Gabe will be, how determined to change my mind. He'd rip me off the Bear trips and consign me to death-by-glare for months. It would definitely mean the end of my aspirations to find a new path for myself.

And all Hanna is really asking me to do is help her find a little happiness that she thoroughly deserves.

"I hate you," I tell her.

"Yeah," she says. "I know. Now. What do we do first?"

I sigh one of those sighs that comes up from your soul.

"Let's start with clothes."

5

———————

HANNA

"**G**randdad." I've accosted him in his favorite rocker on the front porch. "My friend Easton is coming over tonight to help me with some work stuff. Don't give him a hard time. It's not a date."

I'm secretly afraid that my extremely grumpy grandfather will actually get a shotgun out at some point and deal damage to one of the assholes who has passed through my life this year. I try to tell him as little as possible, but somehow—probably because we live in the world's biggest game of telephone, also known as the town of Rush Creek—he always seems to find out.

Like for example, when Nan—who owns Rush Creek bakery—fixed me up with her nephew and he took me geocaching. That part was bad enough, but then it turned out that Nan's nephew was massively socially anxious and had asked his auntie for help. Through the whole (already painful) date, Nan was text-feeding her nephew his lines.

Nan is friends with my Aunt Meryl, who found out about the weird Cyr-Nan-o date and mentioned it to my grandfather, who offered to "have a talk" with Nan's nephew, which I assumed meant break both his kneecaps.

Before that, there was Mack Gault, who I actually kind of liked, until it turned out that he was a semi-retired porn star who wanted to restart his career. His idea was that we could film ourselves getting it on and he could use it as part of his portfolio, to show he still had what it took. I guess the good news is that he went about it in a totally above-board way, asking me to sign a release before he started the cameras, which gave me a chance to tell him he could shove his cameras up his (admittedly very fine) ass.

My grandfather somehow got wind of that, too, and offered to break Mack Gault's kneecaps, which I assumed meant tear him limb from limb and bury the parts on opposite sides of our large ranch.

I assume the women I've dated would be subject to the same outraged treatment—like the one who accidentally told me the wrong time, so I showed up to discover she'd double booked me with another date—but miraculously, that particular story didn't reach my grandfather's ears.

"Easton's one of the Wilder boys, isn't he?" my grandfather asks, adjusting the angle of his rocking chair to catch the last of the late afternoon sun. "The one that dated that girl who made your middle school life hell?"

"Britney Ambrose," I agree.

Britney was the worst of the girls who made me feel like something someone had dragged in on their shoe. Easton's choosing her had, for obvious reasons, rubbed me the wrong way. So, in our early twenties, just when he and I might have outgrown our trash-talking habit and become something like friends for real, I found the perfect reason to keep him at arm's length. Where he's stayed until now.

My granddad's wiry eyebrows draw together. "He's also the one they call the panty melter."

"Jesus, Granddad," I say. "How do you know about that?"

I know my granddad has crossed paths with all the Wilders at one time or another, but I wouldn't have guessed he'd know Easton from any of his brothers—least of all by his reputation.

"Isn't much I don't know," my grandfather says, tipping his cowboy hat a little farther back on his head.

I wonder if he knows that Bear Warden has come to town. If so, I sincerely hope he doesn't know that I've sprung a crush on him. That I've asked Easton to help me "woo him," by which I really mean get close enough to him to win his heart. Or at least his undivided attention, a few dates, and some mountain man nookie.

"Just watch out for Easton," my grandfather says. "Once a panty melter, always a panty melter. Even if this isn't a date, he might still try to melt your panties."

There is nothing grosser than hearing your grandfather say "panty." In an effort to stave off any further panty mentions, I change the subject. "Hey. Did Aunt Meryl talk to you about your birthday party?"

"She did." He squints at me, all leathery rancher skin and spun-sugar old-man hair. Eyes still sharp and a little mean. "Said you needed a guest list and to know what I wanted to eat."

"That's right."

"No pasta and potato salads," he says.

"Yep, know that."

"No Guinness, no whatever those porter-things are. Look like coffee, taste like phlegm."

"Already off the table."

"I don't want to invite people just because they invited us to something. I'm too old for that bullshit. And no birthday cake. Pies."

"How about pies for you to eat, and a birthday cake because everyone else will want to see you blow your candles out?"

"The party's not *for* everyone else, is it?"

I don't try to debate it with him. I've spent a lifetime of meeting his stubborn with my stubborn, so I know my best bet is to just quietly serve cake alongside his precious pies.

He shrugs. "I told Aunt Meryl no birthday cake, too. Figured if I told you both, more chance one of you would listen."

"Or we'd gang up on you and ignore you," I offer.

He flattens his mouth before a smile can creep out, then jabs a finger in my direction.

"And I want the boys there."

My hand, reaching for my phone to take notes, stills. "The boys."

"Your brothers."

The mention of my brothers, as always, makes my stomach hurt.

"We can invite them," I say slowly, "but I don't know that you should get your hopes up that they'll show up."

"Buncha stubborn, proud…"

He's getting himself riled up. "We can ask," I repeat. "I'll reach out to them."

I grew up surrounded by my brothers, the runt of a rowdy otherwise-all-male litter, fighting for my survival but also always knowing I was loved. Then my family fell apart, in stages and degrees, and my brothers all fled Rush Creek at the earliest opportunity available to them.

Part of me is still hurt at getting left behind.

And all of me is sure none of my brothers are gonna show up for my grandfather's birthday party.

"You tell them I said to get their asses out here."

"Sure, Granddad. I'll do that."

"I'm not gonna live forever you know. I'm eighty-fucking-five. And when I go, I want you to have family."

"I have Aunt Meryl."

"Aunt Meryl," he scoffs. "And her twenty-two cats in her falling-down house. No. I want you to have family that can take care of you."

"I don't need taking care of. And I have the Wilders."

"They're not family," he says. "They can fire you."

Okay, technically, that's true. And sometimes it does bother me. I'm *not* a Wilder, and I never will be, so no matter how much they try to make me feel like one of the family, I'm just... not.

For some reason, I think of Easton, age nine, pressing flat stones into my palm. The weight holding me to earth so I wouldn't fly apart into a million pieces.

"We had another offer to buy," my granddad says.

"Yeah? What is it this time?"

"Uranium mining company."

I raise my eyebrows. "You thinking about it?"

"No fucking way."

Our family has lived for a hundred years on this land,

sprawling grasslands separated by scrub and occasional windbreaks. Ranch barns and outbuildings squat here and there, beside a pond or two, the southern edge hemmed by a river, the whole territory capped with a ranch house I've heard called "charming."

We haven't run the ranch as a working ranch in years, not since we sold off the last of our cattle and horses to pay my granddad's medical bills after he had heart surgery almost a decade ago. Since then, he's kept us going by renting out the stables, barns, outbuildings, and kennels, letting local companies park trailers and run businesses on the land, leasing water rights, and allowing small-scale mining of gemstones in exchange for a share of profits.

My grandfather's entertained plenty of offers to sell… but he never goes through with it. Usually that's because the offer's from a company that would destroy the land.

But sometimes the offer's just "not good enough," and I'm sure it's because he still believes one of his grandkids will want the land. He knows I don't. As much as I love it, I've spent enough of my adult life hassling with it. But I'm pretty sure he's still convinced my brothers are coming back. And that when they do, they'll want the ranch.

I think he's delusional, but that's a fight I'm not gonna pick with an eighty-five-year-old grouch.

Luckily, I'm saved from further discussions of birthday parties, uranium mining, or panties by the sound of a car taking the final bend in our long driveway. Easton's red Jeep comes into view.

"On the other hand, maybe you should date him," my granddad says. "That's a nice car."

6

———

EASTON

I've never been inside the house where Hanna lives with her grandfather. I approach it up a long, winding driveway through pale brown and sage green high desert, and park by the garage—which looks newer than the house.

As I near the porch, I find Hanna sitting next to an old man—slightly stooped, white-haired, and sharp-eyed. I've never talked to her grandfather—he's a bit of a loner—but I've seen him around town.

He gets to his feet over my protests that he doesn't need to.

"It's a Friday night," he says, squinting at me. "What are you doing with my granddaughter on a Friday night, if it's not a date?"

"Granddad!" Hanna cries.

Somehow, I don't think Hanna wants me to tell him we're going to assess her wardrobe, so I say, "We're co-leading some trips and we have some planning to do." It's a version of the truth I can live with.

"I told you not to give him a hard time, Granddad," Hanna says sternly from behind him. "Let him in, come on."

He holds out his hand, and I take it. Despite his age and the somewhat gnarled state of his fingers, he has a strong grip. I would have expected no less.

"Fox Hott," he says. "And don't bother making jokes. Those were old when I was sixteen."

"Nice to meet you," I tell him.

He scowls at me—a facial expression so familiar it gives me a jolt. Now, at least, I know where Hanna gets it.

"Don't make me give you a hard time," he growls.

"Granddad," Hanna says.

"Yes?"

"Can it."

Swallowing a laugh, I follow Hanna into the house.

"Nice place." I'm standing inside a massive great room with high ceilings, thick beams, and a huge stone fireplace. Two of the room's three walls are mostly windows, and the dramatic views of the Cascades temporarily silence me. I've loved the mountains and woods since I was a baby, but I can still be awed when I see them from a new perspective.

"Pretty, right?" Hanna says.

"God. Beautiful."

I drag my gaze back inside. At some point, someone put a lot of work into decorating this room with big comfy furniture, throw pillows, and fringed blankets, but it's seen better days.

"This way." She tips her head.

I follow her down a hall and into a room. The bed is made with a simple navy bedspread. The walls are white, with a few unframed vintage ski posters and a couple of National Park maps. Aside from the bed, there's a bookcase full of paperbacks, mostly mysteries and thrillers, and a nightstand with an alarm clock and a water bottle.

A terrarium on top of the bookcase holds the leopard gecko I pranked her with on her birthday.

"You kept him."

She frowns. "I mean, what else would I have done with him? This isn't his habitat."

That's so Hanna.

The whole room is so Hanna. Practical, unassuming, no frills.

And then I spot the pink teddy bear, propped very carefully in the middle of the pillow. I snatch him up.

She snatches him back. "Leave Leonard alone."

"Leonard, huh?" For whatever reason, I'm thoroughly charmed by this proof of life. "He's *pink*."

"The room used to be pink," Hanna says.

"I can't imagine you in a pink room."

"I hated it." She's got that far-off gaze again. "One day when my dad was around and my mom was out with friends, he asked me if I wanted to paint it a different color, and I said yes. So, we did. But I sometimes feel bad I didn't just leave it. She was so crushed when she saw what we'd done, and what the hell difference would it have made? The pink had made her so happy." Her gaze sharpens to the present and finds my face. She shrugs. "It's just a color. Anyway. Here's my closet."

She gets up from the bed and opens a set of double doors to reveal the contents of her wardrobe.

"And the rest of my stuff is in here."

She points to a serviceable oak dresser with plain wooden drawer pulls.

"Bear's going to be at the Wilder offices all day on Monday, meeting with us and Gabe to debrief the first trip and try to refine some stuff. I want to use that opportunity to look unforgettable." She scowls at her clothes. "So no baggy sweatshirts and jeans."

"Show me what you've got."

She starts pulling out clothes and tossing them on the bed. "Baggy. Baggy, baggy, baggy, baggy."

"I'm sensing a theme. What do you wear on dates?"

She pulls out a scoop-necked black top.

"Let's see."

"Hang on," she says, and steps out of the room. I hear a door closing down the hall and assume it's the bathroom.

When she steps back in, she's still wearing jeans, but her sweatshirt has been replaced by the black top.

She looks fantastic.

Her skin is pale, her cheeks pinked from the quick clothing swap. The black of the top sets off the black of her hair, and her blue-green eyes are vivid against the black-and-white background.

And then there's the top. Body-hugging, low-cut, clinging to Hanna's generous body, revealing the smooth white heaped-up curves of her delicious-looking tits.

It's not like I've never seen Hanna in anything form fitting. There have been a couple of occasions, including Gabe's wedding, but they've always been whirlwinds of family distraction.

I've never seen her standing across from me, hands on hips, modeling her spectacular Hanna-ness for me, with nowhere for me to put my gaze except on her full-blown curves.

"Is it awful?" she asks. "You look a little shell-shocked."

"No—sorry—my mind just went somewhere else. It looks good on you."

Her eyes open a little at that, and her lips twitch. Then she shrugs. "No worries," she says.

She turns half away from me, which makes things slightly worse, because she has a truly mouth-watering ass. How have I missed this fact? I guess because she is not a tall woman, and she wears sweatshirts that are big enough to cover large swaths of her.

"I don't think I can wear this to work," she says.

I shake my head in agreement. "I mean, you could, but..."

It's very distracting, I don't finish.

I mean, for one thing, it's super sexist. Women shouldn't have to dress in a way that keeps men from being uncomfortable.

But also, I don't want to make things weird by making Hanna think about how I'm thinking about...

"It'll look like I'm trying too hard," she finishes for me.

Not what I was going to say, but it'll do the trick. "Yes. That."

"Basically, I have two kinds of clothes. Trying hard clothes and not trying at all clothes. I need a middle category."

"Trying but not looking like you're trying clothes."

"Right, exactly." She pins me with a look, and I have the distinct feeling I'm not going to love what's coming next.

"We're going shopping."

7

HANNA

The next morning, Easton picks me up and we drive out of town to my favorite swank mall.

"I still think this is a terrible idea," he says.

"What is?" I ask. Because so far nothing strikes me as particularly terrible. It was a little weird having Easton in my bedroom, but once I got used to it, it wasn't a big deal.

It was definitely a lot weird having Easton assessing my clothing choices, staring at my boobs and ass, but I didn't hate it. He was nice about it, which itself is weird, because Easton and I don't do nice.

"I hate shopping," Easton says.

"I hate shopping, too," I point out.

"So why did you suggest it?"

"Because it's still the most efficient way to acquire new belongings."

"Right," he says.

"Okay. We're over that objection, right?"

"Yes, but..."

"But what?"

"I just think this won't be good for our friendship."

I turn to stare at him.

He turns and meets my startled gaze. "What?"

"You said we're friends."

"Duh, Hanna, obviously we're friends."

I hide a smile. "You've just never said it."

"We've been friends for like thirty years," he says, like this whole conversation is absurd.

But it's not. I *like* it. I like that Easton just said that we're friends. Guys don't say stuff like that very often, so you have to really soak it up when they do.

"You sticky-noted my entire cube from top to bottom," he says. "Would you do that for someone who wasn't your friend?"

"Absolutely," I say. "If I thought it would annoy them, and I wanted to get their goat? No doubt."

"Okay, let me check my assumptions here, then," he says. "I thought the fact that you sticky-noted my cube and brought me donuts meant that we were friends. Even if you ate five-thirteenths of my donuts. I thought that meant you felt comfortable enough with me as a friend to eat five-thir-teenths of my birthday donuts."

"We *are* friends," I say. "It's just that the sticky-notes aren't foolproof evidence of it."

"You're impossible."

I hide another smile. "Why do you think shopping with me will be bad for our friendship?"

"Because if I tell you something looks awful on you, you'll get your feelings hurt."

"I won't. I promise."

"Everyone always says that," he grumbles. "But no one actually wants honesty."

"I do."

The corner of his mouth turns up. "I guess I believe that."

Despite his protests, Easton steers us faithfully to the mall, and we arrive at my favorite store, the one I basically never allow myself to shop at because leggings cost more than a hundred dollars there.

But I've decided that the mission to make Bear Warden fall in love with me is worth some wild spending.

And the universe rewards me for this thinking, because when we step through the door, a saleswoman greets us.

"Hello!" she says. "You may or may not know this, but today is *member day!* And that means twenty percent off everything and forty percent off if you open a credit card with us today. Plus ten percent off on top of that if the item is marked with a pink dot."

"Whoa," I say.

"So, pick out everything you want to see your girlfriend in," she teases Easton.

We both freeze.

"Not her/my girlfriend/boyfriend," we say at the same time.

"Oh, gosh! I'm sorry. That was—you know what they say, about 'assume' making an aaaa—you get the gist," she sputters, turning red.

"No worries," we say at the same time.

I duck away and start sifting through clothes on the nearest rack.

"There are no men's clothes in here," Easton says.

"Nope," I say.

"So I…"

"Just stand there and look pretty."

"Right," he says.

For some reason, I take a peek behind me, as if it's necessary to confirm that he is, in fact, looking pretty.

He is.

I mean, Easton always looks good. He's a Wilder. He's six-foot-plus with great hair, longish in his case, and a sculpted nose and jaw, and his mom's beautiful green eyes. He's a little leaner than Gabe and Clark, but still built in a way that makes the Wilder Adventures t-shirt he's wearing cling like a second skin to his pecs and biceps. And don't get me started on how flattering those jeans are on him.

"You're doing a good job," I inform him.

He looks confused, and I don't clarify.

I fill my arms with clothes, which causes a saleswoman to materialize from nowhere and carry them off to the dressing room.

When I'm done emptying all the clothes racks in the store, I drag Easton to the dressing room with me.

"Can he come in with me?" I ask the saleswoman who's guarding the entryway to the dressing room area—not the one who greeted us or the one who portaged my clothes.

"Definitely." She produces a folding stool from a small stack leaning against the wall and sets it up opposite the curtains that hide my dressing room from public view. "We encourage boyfriends and husbands."

We've learned our lesson and don't bother correcting her.

SHOPPING WITH EASTON turns out to be far different from what I was expecting.

I had pictured him leaning against the wall with a bored expression on his face, grudgingly passing judgment on me, my body, and fashion choices in an effort to keep me from ratting him out to Gabe.

Instead, I've discovered that what Easton means by "I hate shopping" is very different from what I mean.

"Too big," he says, shaking his head when I show him the first outfit. "You need at least one size smaller."

"This is my size."

He shakes his head. "Stay right there."

He's back a minute or two later with smaller sizes. "And I found this, too," he says. "The shirt looks like something you'd like, and these leggings were with it, so I grabbed them." He surveys the clothes already hanging in the dressing room. "That tank top will work," he says, pointing.

He yanks the curtain closed between us, dismissing me before I can object.

"Hidden talents," I call to him. "Do your brothers know?"

"They know I can dress myself, unlike certain other Wilder brothers, who never wear anything except base layers, wool sweaters, and hiking pants."

It's true that Easton is the snappiest dresser—well, the only dresser who could reasonably be categorized as snappy—in the Wilder crew. Unlike his brothers, when he's off duty, he usually wears jeans and a button-down. While theoretically I don't give a shit what Easton wears, I have once or twice noticed that his clothes flatter his frame.

And he definitely has a knack for choosing jeans that draw attention to his ass...ets.

Needless to say, I would never tell him this, because it would give him a big(ger) head.

I try on the outfit that Easton picked out. It's a pair of dusty-rose yoga pants and a black tank top. They're much more form-fitting than anything else I've chosen. Part of me wants to pull them off instead of showing Easton, but the whole point of this enterprise is to get things that aren't baggy, right?

And I don't give a crap what Easton thinks, anyway.

I sweep the curtains open.

"Do you think he wants to see this much of me? Does anyone want to see this much of me?"

Although in truth, I'm fascinated by how I look. Round, curvy, and real.

I kind of can't take my eyes off myself. Look at me, people!

Look at me, Bear Warden! I dare you to look away.

If I'd known how awesome ridiculously expensive clothes could be, I would have spent more money on them sooner.

I twirl in front of the mirror, assessing, then look up to find Easton's eyes on my reflection.

"The whole world definitely wants to see that much of you."

His voice sounds just-woken-up rough, and he clears his throat.

I tip my head, trying to gauge if he's teasing or not, but

my Easton mockery radar doesn't blip. I think he's just being charming, because Easton is extremely good at that. He basically can't help himself, which is why he almost got beaten up by Gabe when Lucy first came on the scene and by Kane when Mari did.

"Try that purple thing with it," he says, pointing to a drapey purple thing.

I do. It's basically like a baggy sweatshirt, except somehow... hotter. It's tight in the arms and exposes my collarbones and everything from the belly button down.

I look *good*.

Easton's eyes snag mine in the mirror, then fall away before I can think about that too much.

"Okay," I say, turning to face him. "I'm going to wear this on Monday, and then I'm going to—what? What am I going to do? Trip and fall in his lap? Ask him if he wants to get naked with me on the next hike?"

The corner of Easton's mouth turns up. "There might be a subtler first step," he allows.

"Right, this is why you're helping me! I need strategy. I look superhot, he stares at me longingly, and then... I...?" I open my palms.

"Ask him out."

"To...?"

Easton mulls this. "Drinks? Dinner? A hike? Could be anything."

"This is all assuming that the outfit does its job," I say.

"That outfit..."

His eyes rake over me, and I brace for at best neutral appraisal, at worst judgment, but I get neither. Instead, his gaze warms with approval, clinging to my curves, setting off a blaze of liquid heat in my body. My body stretches and purrs like a kitten under his regard.

Whoa.

Wait.

That…

But before I can think too much about the meaning of his gaze or my reaction, Easton coughs and starts again. "That outfit is just fine. Assuming Bear Warden isn't an idiot."

"He's not an idiot," I say.

He frowns. "You've known him, how long, a couple weeks? He's still showing you his best self. Wait and see."

"You sound like you want him to turn out to be a dick."

"No, of course I don't. It's just…"

But he doesn't finish.

I return to admiring my outfit.

"If I ever wear this in the woods, it'll get ruined," I say, idly running my hands over the sleek fabric clutching my thighs. The leggings are made from something soft and delicate, and I keep touching.

His eyes follow my hands.

"You need different underwear under that," he says, his voice steady and cool.

I shrug. "See? I knew you were the best man for this job. I'll get different underwear." I point a finger at him. "Which I can do without your help. But I'm definitely buying this outfit. Right? I mean, it works, right?"

Our eyes meet in the mirror. His drop away.

"Yeah," he says. "It works."

8

HANNA

After the first outfit is such a success, I send him back to find me more things I wouldn't have chosen for myself. And he appoints himself Guy Who Gets the Right Size. Even when it means having to ask the saleswomen for help.

Needless to say, the saleswomen *love* helping Easton. The ones who haven't already clocked us together flirt shamelessly with him, and one gives him her phone number.

"Jesus, Easton!" I whisper when he shows me. "You can't help yourself!"

"I didn't *do* anything," he whispers back.

"Nooo," I say. "You didn't give her the thousand-watt smile and the green-eyed gaze of seduction, and you didn't ask her name and you didn't thank her like she'd just gone down on you in a—"

I'd been about to say *dressing room* but that feels a little close to home for some reason, so I cut myself off.

Still, Easton's eyes widen.

"You, Hanna Hott," he says. "How have I known you for basically thirty years and you are just now revealing the extent of your depravity?"

"It took me this long to reach this fever pitch of sexual deprivation," I inform him.

A strange expression crosses Easton's face.

"You still have one more to try on," he says, voice rough again, and slides the curtain shut between us.

When I'm done trying things on, I make Easton help me narrow down my choices, then load up my credit card.

"Burritos?" I ask, heading toward the food court without waiting for an answer.

"Hell yes," he says.

"You didn't even work up the appetite."

He narrows his eyes at me. "I carried clothes back and forth for you. You just stood there looking superhot."

That expression, "superhot," was originally my own, but it still catches me off guard in Easton's mouth. I feel like I've been dipped in molten chocolate, but I pretend to be normal-Hanna and raise my eyebrows at him.

"What?" He sounds extremely grumpy about it, which I totally understand. If our situations were reversed and I had to pay him a compliment, even one that was just a repeat of what he'd already said, I would also begrudge it. "You said it. And it's, objectively, true."

This doesn't help with the molten chocolate problem, and I scan his face for signs that he's messing with me, but he just rolls his eyes.

"Right," I say.

We order our burritos and scarf them at a table in the

food court, surrounded by my shopping bags and a large number of middle-aged women.

"Are we done?" Easton asks, after we throw away our wrappers.

"No."

"*I* think we're done."

"We're not."

"You can't *carry* more clothes," he says.

That's demonstrably *not true*, but I don't argue with him. I just start walking.

He heaves an enormous sigh but follows me.

I stop outside J.J. Brewer, which sells clothes that look like they were stolen straight from Easton's closet. "Your turn."

"My turn for what?"

"To try something on."

He side-eyes me.

"Come on."

"To review: I hate shopping."

"For someone who hates shopping, you sure did seem to be enjoying yourself."

He screws up his face, but follows me in.

I succeed in convincing him to try on a few things—a pair of dark jeans, a t-shirt that's almost the same color as his eyes, a silver-y button-down.

He comes out of the dressing room to show me.

"What's it like?" I ask him.

"What?" he asks, looking down at himself.

"Being disgustingly good-looking? Having women write their phone numbers on your arm? Getting laid on the regular?"

"I take it that means the clothes look okay," he says dryly.

"They don't suck," I say.

This is a ridiculous understatement. The jeans look like they were stitched from a model of his body. The t-shirt hugs his pecs and cuffs his biceps. His hair is a little rumpled from the undressing and dressing, which gives him that bed-head charm that I know—from a lifetime of watching from the sidelines—no woman can resist.

"You probably have a six-pack under there, too," I say, disgusted. And yet, not actually disgusted. Quite the opposite. I have to admit, getting Easton to try on clothes is a purely selfish act. It's like having my very own Extremely Sexy Paper Doll.

After he checks out, as we're walking back to the car, I ask him a question I've been meaning to throw at him ever since I overheard him and Bear in the conference room.

"Hey, Easton?"

"Yeah?"

"Why do you want to leave Wilder and work for Bear? You have employment for life, great co-workers, the dream gig."

His stride hitches, like I've caught him way off guard. I guess we don't have a lot of real conversations, so I get that.

For a moment, I think he's not planning to answer, but then he takes a breath.

"You know how many times I've mentioned to Gabe that I know we can get more mileage out of our social media? So, what does he do? Instead of letting me take it and run with it, he and Lucy hire Bear Warden. We could have *been* Bear Warden if he'd taken me seriously."

"Maybe he didn't realize you wanted to take it on. I feel like every time it's come up, you've had a lot on your plate already."

He shakes his head. "It just doesn't even cross his mind that I can do it. You know how it is, being the youngest."

He stops then and looks at me. "Maybe it's different because you're the girl. And because your brothers aren't all still here."

I take the small hit in my breastbone like a champ. I know he didn't say it to be hurtful; no one knows how much it wounds that my brothers left me behind, and if I have my way, no one ever will.

Easton hitches a shoulder. "But for me, I've been trying to carve out something that feels like mine, really *mine*, the way the others have. Seeing Kane figure it out last year, I don't know—it just kind of lit a fire for me. I don't want to just accept Gabe's version of me anymore. I want to work with someone who will take me seriously."

Most of the time, when Easton talks, it's teasing, and most of the time I'm hunting for the perfect comeback, but this feels different. I haven't really ever heard Easton talk about himself, and it's moving. I know he and I are both the youngest, and of course I know all the ways that's hard— but I guess I never thought much about how it was hard, specifically, for Easton.

It's funny that he's such a jokester at the same time he longs to be taken seriously. I wonder why he does that, jokes around so much.

Maybe it's the only role his family has ever really given him.

I realize that at some point we stopped walking and are

just standing at the edge of the parking lot. Easton's watching my face, like he's gauging whether I'm about to start making fun of him.

On any other day, I would, for sure, but he's just done something nice for me, and I don't feel like it right now.

"And Bear does? Take you seriously?" I ask, instead.

"So far, yes. He's been looking at my reels and YouTube videos, telling me what works and what doesn't, giving me advice, helping me with stuff I'm interested in."

"Huh," I say.

"Huh what?" he says.

"I guess—it's not so different from my reasons for liking Bear."

"You like that he takes you seriously?" Easton asks.

I don't want to go into it right now, the maybe-it-wouldn't-suck-to-be-treated-like-a-princess thing. I just shrug.

Easton looks like he wants to say something, but he doesn't. He just says, "Huh."

And we start walking again.

9

———

EASTON

I have spent way, way more time than is reasonable or appropriate or healthy trying to figure out what Hanna is wearing under the new outfit I sort of picked out for her.

Gabe, Bear, Hanna, and I are sitting around the conference table, debriefing the first trip. It's mostly pro forma—things went pretty well.

Which leaves a little too much time for my mind to wander.

Those pants. I guess they're technically yoga pants? Or flowy leggings? Is that a thing? They're fitted at the top and wide at the bottom, a dusty rose color that reminds me of the color Hanna's cheeks turned the other day when she blushed.

I have obviously broken something crucial in my brain because *none* of what is in it right now makes one iota of sense.

I was unable to stop thinking about Hanna for the rest of the weekend after our shopping trip. Hanna preening.

Hanna enjoying her hot self in the mirror. Hanna's tits and ass and pussy revealed by the tight clothes I'd stupidly, foolishly, self-destructively, suggested that she put on in order to win over Bear Warden.

On Saturday night, I may or may not have lost a very serious battle with myself over whether it was wrong to jerk off in the shower while thinking about Hanna stretching and twirling and then—in my fantasy—turning to me to ask, "Do you like it, Easton? Do you like the way I look?" in a purring voice.

And then going down on me in...

...a dressing room.

Hanna.

Hanna Hott.

What *is* this madness?

I mean, it's not like I've never had a sexual thought about Hanna before.

I just try really, really hard not to, because she's my co-worker and my friend and it's inconvenient. So, in the past, if I've found myself noticing her body or getting hard while I'm bantering with her (which maybe happens every once in a while, inexplicably), I just remind myself of what a complete pain in the ass she is, and also that she thinks I'm a complete pain in the ass. And if neither of those things works, I think about what Gabe would say if I touched a hair on Hanna's head.

None of those tricks is working today.

"Thoughts on what could work *more* smoothly?" Bear asks us, derailing my inappropriate thought train.

"Oh, dang, I left my notes in my cube," Hanna says. "I'll be right back."

She shoves her chair out and heads away from us.

I try not to go another round on the is-she-isn't-she game, but in an effort not to try to catch another glimpse of Hanna's glorious, heart-shaped ass, I find myself watching Bear.

Who's watching Hanna.

Not like a drooling asshole. Just taking little bite-sized glances. Most men twelve and up have successfully trained themselves not to ogle, and Bear is no exception, but I'm also a man, and I know their tricks. Peripheral vision and scanning the room as if looking for something else. And then the occasional slightly longer glance, just to satisfy the craving.

I should be ecstatic for my friend Hanna, who has accomplished *exactly* what she wanted to with those skin-tight yoga pants or whatever the fuck they are. But instead, I'm experiencing above-average amounts of anger—at the pants. And toward myself for bringing them to her.

And again toward myself, for saying that thing about the underwear.

Because if she had panty lines, I would not be thinking, *Is she?*

Or isn't she?

And if she isn't, how does the fabric feel against her body?

Is it snug against her pussy?

Does it feel good?

It took me this long to reach this fever pitch of sexual deprivation.

What, exactly does that *mean*?

"—thoughts on that, Easton?" Gabe asks.

"I—I'm sorry," I say. "I was thinking about something else."

He raises his eyebrows. "I asked what your thoughts were about any additional obstacles we need to take into account when we do the rafting version of Bear's workshop."

Hanna comes back to the table with her notes and plops into her seat. "The only thing I really noted was that" —she turns to Bear—"we need to start cooking earlier. By the time we ate, I could have torn a rabbit apart with my bare hands and eaten it bloody."

I snort. Bear looks a little taken aback.

See, this. This is exactly what I meant when I said she shouldn't think about changing herself for him. If he can't appreciate her blunt, colorful way of talking, then...

Fuck him.

No, no. I don't mean that. Hanna takes a little getting used to, and Bear is demonstrably a good guy. If he weren't, Hanna wouldn't be interested.

"What if we keep the rafting or the hike—whichever we're doing on a given trip—relatively short?" Hanna continues. "Then you'd have more time for the meat of the workshop."

"Makes total sense to me," Bear says, recovering and smiling at her. "The other thing I'd love to do next time is get both of you on camera more. I know you were basically just learning the drill the first trip, but next time I want you and Easton to get a chance to shine."

"I don't care if I get camera time," Hanna says. "I want to learn how to forage and cook so I can add those elements to

Wilder's other offerings. Don't you think that would be cool, Gabe?"

Hanna, ever the diplomat.

"We should probably talk about that another time, Han," Gabe says, giving Bear a wry no-we-aren't-openly-discussing-stealing-your-workshop glance.

"It's fine," Bear says. "If I can be useful to you guys that way, I'm happy to. And Hanna, I'd be delighted to share what I know with you. I'm looking forward to it, in fact."

Hanna beams at him.

He beams back.

I resist the urge to smack my head on the conference table.

Barely.

MY SISTER AMANDA SHOWS UP, as she does almost daily, with lunch. Amanda, who's the next older sibling than me and the only Wilder girl, runs a catering service called Around the Table, and one of her gigs is feeding us lunch every day. When she can, she shows up in person with the food and eats with us.

Today it's Cuban rice and black beans. Around the Table's lunch offerings have gotten extra delicious in the last few years, since Rachel, who's Cuban-American, and Jessa, who's Korean-American, started dating my brothers Brody and Clark. I mean, don't get me wrong, I love a good pasta bake—but the Perez's rice and beans and Jessa's family's soft tofu stew have been welcome additions to the lunch menu.

In addition to the regular staff—aka my brothers—lunch time often brings a raft of other Wilder family and friends—mostly girlfriends, wives, husbands, and kids. There's a mob today, everyone descending on the offices from their various day jobs. Cuban food day tends to do that.

Today's lunch mob crowds the table, jostling and joking, until they all remember we have a guest and step aside to let Bear to grab his food first.

Hanna's the last one to get the memo. I'm standing too far away to nudge her, and she's about to scoop a huge helping of rice and beans onto her plate when she looks up and sees that everyone else has drawn back.

Her face turns red.

See, that's the thing about Hanna. She's blunt and no-holds-barred, and she can put her foot in it, but I think sometimes she just doesn't know how to play the game. Or she's in her own head and can't see that there's even a game in progress.

I know she's embarrassed, and I want to come up with a way for her to save face.

My way, I admit it, will probably involve giving her shit so she can give me shit back and we can both walk away from it laughing.

But what happens instead is that Bear gently takes the scoop from Hanna's hand and fills her plate for her.

And Hanna turns even more red.

I'm torn between gratitude toward Bear for rescuing her, and irritation. Because Bear's assistant, Cypress, is filming the whole scene, and I know that's part of why Bear did it. Because he's got this gallant guy role thing, and Hanna provides him with a chance to play it to the hilt.

But there's nothing I can do about it. I'm not exactly going to call him out on it, and being nice on camera isn't a sin—so I just get in line and grab my lunch.

By the time I get my food, Bear is surrounded by Wilders, laughing and talking and answering questions.

Amanda is the only one standing aside, setting out dessert on a card table she uses for that purpose. I drift her way, and she smiles at me.

"I guess Bear was a good bet," she says. "The response to the first workshop was phenomenal. Everyone likes him."

"Yeah," I say.

Her eyebrows go up. "Do I detect some reticence?"

"He's very... camera-ready," I murmur.

"That he is," she says appreciatively.

I scowl.

"What's your problem with him?" she asks. "Even Hanna likes him."

"I don't have a problem with him. I just don't think he's necessarily as all-that as some people think he is."

"Okay," she says slowly. Her eyebrows draw together.

I don't like that look on her. It's her thinking look. Her figuring-it-out look.

For whatever stupid reason, I don't want to be figured out right now.

At all.

10

HANNA

Bear leaves right after lunch, saying he and Cypress have to go edit some footage.

Amanda plops down in the seat next to me, and our other friends start pulling up chairs.

Amanda and I haven't been friends since elementary school, the way Easton and I have. Our families weren't crazy close or anything, so she and I didn't really get to know each other until I went to work for Wilder. And even then, it wasn't like we clicked and suddenly it was all sleepover parties and doing each other's hair. (For one thing, mine's too short, but also, I don't do girl bonding that way. Like I told Easton, too many feelings and too much probing and someone always ends up in tears.)

But Amanda is no-bullshit in a way I like, and she's crazy about her family, which obviously I am too, and after a while we just started hanging out a bunch. Then Lucy came to town and fell for Gabe, and Rachel came *back* to town and fell for Brody, and Jessa, who was already *in* town, fell for Clark, and Mari, who was supposed to just be passing through, fell for Kane.

So now there's this whole girl posse. And most of the time it's fine, but... I don't know. Sometimes I feel like I'm on the outside looking in. Even when, like now, I'm the one they've circled around.

"He's *dreamy*," Amanda says

There's a round of nods and heated agreement from the others.

"Those *thighs*," Lucy says. This is understandable because Gabe and Clark both have tree-trunk thighs.

"That *beard*," Jessa says. Also on brand, because Jessa is with Clark, the Viking.

"I *heard that*," Clark says from somewhere nearby. "I also have a very good beard!"

We all ignore him.

"That *voice*," Rachel says.

We all turn to look at her. Brody has a deep voice, but he's not a bass.

"What?" she says. "A woman can appreciate the other options, can't she?"

"Oh, hell, yes," Amanda says. "We can definitely appreciate. Hanna, are you appreciating?"

"I'd have to be dead not to," I say, although this makes me feel just a tiny, tiny bit *weird*.

Because.

Because of this thing I did.

"Any particular area of appreciation?" Rachel inquires.

"Mmm," I say. "All of the above."

It's true. I appreciate the beard and the thighs and the voice. A lot.

"New outfit?" Amanda asks, inadvertently striking at the heart of my weird feelings.

"Uh, yeah."

The women exchange a round of glances.

"It's just a new outfit," I say. "I just needed something new."

"Uh-huh," Amanda says.

"We're not having this conversation," I say.

"Which conversation?" she asks innocently.

"No conversation."

In fairness, although Amanda does her share of match-making and otherwise intruding, I'm usually the one who asks the questions people don't want to answer. For instance, I was the one who stuck my big ol' foot in my mouth and asked Mari—right after she first came to Rush Creek—if she was going to fall in love with a Wilder and stay.

I mean, given all that came before, it was a reasonable question. But probably not one I would have wanted to answer if I were in her shoes.

So they would be well within their rights to question me—do my new clothes mean I intend to lure Bear into falling in love and sticking around?

Not that I delude myself that I could get Bear to stay. I just want to enjoy him while he's here.

They're all watching me intently, and I feel like I'm shrinking under the force of that scrutiny.

Because she's the most loving and forgiving of all of us, Lucy changes the subject. "So," she says. "Kane's photography opening is this weekend! Is he nervous?"

I take advantage of the change of subject to inhale

deeply for the first time in several minutes.

I wasn't lying. I do appreciate the beard, the thighs, and the voice.

When I got home from shopping with Easton on Saturday, I put on my new clothes and looked at myself in the mirror.

I looked *great*.

Even Easton thought so.

The pants clung to my butt and thighs, in the best possible way. And they were so soft. The tank top was made of something super soft, too, and it felt exceptionally good to run my hands over my body through the fabric. Bright and tingly. My nipples were hard and poking through the tank, and I stopped to give them a little attention, and then it would have taken a saint—which I'm not—not to also slide a hand down over my belly to the needy place between my legs. I cupped myself, and the pressure of the elastic cloth and the clutch of my hand were too good to resist.

I thought of Bear—beard, thighs, super appealing dad bod, rumbly voice. I imagined his body moving over mine, his voice in my ear, telling me how good I looked, how good I was making him feel, how good he wanted me to feel.

I must have been primed, because it took me only a minute or two to tease myself right to the edge. All I needed was to grind my palm over the softness, and the voice in my ear would take me over.

Except suddenly it wasn't Bear's voice.

It was Easton's voice.

And I couldn't make his voice, or the tickle of his lips against my ear, or the feel of his lean, hard body against my own, go away, and I came, imagining how his face would look when he thrust inside me.

Then I felt damp and shame-y and had to do laundry so I could wear the new pants today.

It was just the way brains work, though. Just stupid, uncooperative brains.

It didn't *mean* anything.

"Hanna, will you?"

I snap back to reality. "Will I what?"

"I was saying someone should ask Bear to come to the opening," Mari says. "Hanna, will you see him before then? Can you give him an invitation?" She digs around in her purse and pulls out an invitation.

"Sure," I say. Because to refuse would be to court questions, and I really don't want to answer questions.

Also, it occurs to me, invitation in hand, that this might be exactly what I need.

An easy, low-key reason to ask Bear on a date.

Which in turn would be the best possible way to un-weird myself.

11

———————

EASTON

"**H**ey, Easton."

The greeting is wrapped in the smooth, seductive tones of Britney Ambrose, a high school classmate of Hanna's and mine. Britney is absolutely gorgeous in a completely obvious way, like a Victoria's Secret model who lost her way and stumbled into our humble little West-meets-Pacific-Northwest town. Britney and I hooked up during my revolving door phase, and she's been angling for round two ever since.

"Hi, Britney," I say.

I'm out with Clark and Brody at Oscar's Bar and Grill, our favorite haunt. Just a regular old beers-and-burgers thing, dolled up Western style. It comes complete with elk and moose heads over the bar, a saloon door that apparently dates back to, well, saloon days, and a mural on the back wall romanticizing the olden days of Rush Creek, back when cowboys roamed the earth.

Britney gives me a gleaming smile as she toys with her

honey-blond hair. "Long time no see, Easton,"she purrs. "You look great."

"You're looking lovely yourself, Brit."

The words are out of my mouth without thought or plan: Flirting is pretty much an automatic response for me.

Her mouth curves in a sexy little smile. "Aw, thanks. I'm up front at the bar if you feel like stopping by for a drink, or *whatever*, when you're done hanging with your family. Hey, guys," she says, to my brothers, who give her indifferent nods of greeting.

"East," Britney says, touching my arm. "I'll be at the bar. Come find me."

"Sure," I say.

She wafts away from the table, and Brody and Clark smirk at me.

"What?"

"Looks like you have the rest of the evening planned out," Clark says.

I shrug. Britney's attractive, but she's not...

She's not all that. That's what I was going to say.

Brody raises an eyebrow. "No?" he says.

"Just not feelin' it."

Clark is watching me quietly. "You've said that a few times lately."

"It's been true."

Brody chomps the last bite of his burger and swallows a gulp of beer. "Let me take a stab at this. Maybe your sex life is like when you eat too much ice cream and it goes from sweet to bitter?"

"Are you comparing sex to ice cream?"

Brody grins. "I might be."

"Are you implying it's possible to have too much sex? Are you implying I've had too much sex?"

This is pretty ironic because I'm in a dry spell that's lasted…

Well, crap, I don't know how long it's lasted. The last woman I remember sleeping with was a tourist who propositioned me on one of my rafting trips.

It was meh. And it was a *while* ago.

Can't remember the time before that.

Can't remember the last time I had great sex.

How did my sex life become a past-tense blur?

"But it's been a while," I admit. "Six months? Eight months?" I wince. "A year?"

It's possible. That rafting trip was last summer…

"Whoa," Brody says. "That's a long dry spell."

"Go ahead," I say. "Rub it in."

"I think you mean you'll go ahead and rub one out. Another one."

I give him the finger. But he's not wrong. Maybe that's why I'm having trouble keeping Hanna in the box I normally reserve for her. Speaking of rubbing one out.

Or two.

But just two. You could still characterize it as a slip-up, as opposed to a pattern.

I massage my forehead.

Lines form between Clark's eyebrows. "Maybe it's not that you were having too much. Maybe it was that you were having it with the wrong people," he suggests.

"Spoken like a guy who's getting it on the regular with the right person," I say.

Clark struggles, not entirely successfully, not to look smug.

I frown. "I really don't think I'm a guy who has a right person. I've never felt like there was something out there that I needed but couldn't find. Just because you guys are super happy settling down, doesn't mean I would be." I cross my arms.

"You did just say you haven't been happy with the variety super-pack," Clark reminds me.

"Mixing metaphors," Brody scolds. "We were doing ice cream."

Still, Clark has a point. "Maybe the problem is Rush Creek. Maybe I've—to extend your miserable metaphor— tasted all the flavors?"

Hmm. This is another good reason that finding a new path for myself would be great. I could tell Bear that I'm open to spending some chunks of time on site in Colorado, and...

I wince as my brain finishes, *open a different variety super-pack.*

And for a guy who has always enjoyed the variety super-pack, that idea is not nearly as appealing as I would have expected.

12

HANNA

I t takes me a couple of days to get up the courage to invite Bear to Kane's photo exhibit opening.

And it's possible I wouldn't have gotten up the courage at all, except that I run into him in the Wilder parking lot, just as I'm getting out of my truck.

I'd tossed the invitations on my passenger seat, and I grab one as I slide out of the driver's seat.

"Hey!" I call out. Magically, my voice comes out confident and casual. "Has anyone asked you yet if you want to come to Kane's photo exhibit opening? No pressure, but it should be a fun night. You survived lunch with the whole crew the other day, and this should be a little lower key. Fewer kids, more art."

"I like art," Bear says. He smiles at me—big blue, long-lashed eyes, white teeth in that reddish beard—and I wait for my heartbeat to kick up like it did when I first saw him. Maybe the heart can't sustain that kind of adrenaline rush, though, because my pulse stays even. "Is this landscape photography?"

"A lot of it is." I nod. "Some portraits, too, and naked pictures of his girlfriend when she was pregnant."

Whoops, that was probably not a necessary embellishment.

But Bear doesn't seem judgy. "Will you be there?"

"Yeah."

"Then I'll be there."

I'm still examining myself for signs of excitement, so it takes me a moment to realize I need to actually *express* some.

"Uh. Yeah. Then. We'll both be there. That'll be... cool."

God, Hanna. Any dorkier?

"Bear!" Gabe calls out, appearing from headquarters. "Just the man I was looking for. Coupla questions for you."

"See you there, then?" Bear asks.

"See you there."

He takes a step toward Gabe, then turns back and smiles at me.

"I'm really looking forward to it."

"Are you wearing makeup?" Easton demands as he approaches.

It's Kane's opening, and I'm wearing a red top that Easton plucked off a rack for me. I even let Lucy do my makeup.

I panic. "Is it bad? I told Lucy to make it look natural."

I can't read the expression on Easton's face at all. "It's fine," he says. "It looks... pretty."

Pretty is such a weird word. If you say it too many

times, it stops sounding like it means anything. But also, it's a very small, very soft word that, on the face of it, doesn't seem like it should carry a lot of weight. It's not like "superhot."

Except for some reason, "pretty," in Easton's mouth, in reference to me, feels like a lit fuse, in a way that "superhot" just didn't.

I'm being so weird lately. So, so weird. I really need to shake it off and focus on the task at hand, which is to spend time with Bear.

"Thanks," I say. "You don't have to boost my ego as part of the deal."

"Oh, really?" says Easton. "That's good to know." He sticks his tongue out at me. "Because I was staying up nights thinking up ways to do that." He strokes an imaginary beard—Easton is the Wilder most likely to be clean-shaven—and muses. "'Shall I compare thee to a summer's day?'"

I smack his arm. "I bet that's the only line from that poem you know."

"You got me," he admits.

"So," I lower my voice again. "I'm here. Bear's here." I gesture to where he's standing, having just come through the front door of the gallery. "Now what?"

Easton crosses his arms. "I bet you can figure this out for yourself."

"But I'm paying you the big bucks to figure it out for me."

"You're blackmailing me," he reminds me. "And teach a woman to fish, and…"

"She can catch a Bear?"

Easton snorts. "Precisely. Maybe you need to ask yourself what, I don't know, Daphne Bridgerton would do?"

I squint suspiciously at him. "What do *you* know about Daphne Bridgerton?"

Is it my imagination, or does a blush creep over Easton's face? "Nothing," he says. "Only that Amanda can't stop talking about her."

"I don't think Daphne Bridgerton should be my role model here! There's no way I'm taking romantic advice from someone who allowed herself to be laced into a corset and had to have masturbation explained to her on a walk in a park."

Easton makes a small noise that I can't interpret.

"Although it worked, didn't it? I should try it." I lower my voice further. "Hey, Bear. So, there's this thing I've been wondering... what *do* married people do in bed?"

"Don't. Do. That."

"I was just *joking*. Do you really think I'm that hopeless? Don't answer that. I know what sex is. I've even had it. It's just been a long time. Not a long time since I masturbated," I say hastily. Ah, nice, Hanna. I can feel my cheeks getting pink. "Just a long time since—" I stop because there's no way this gets any better.

Easton has a strangled look on his face.

"I'll just shut up now," I say.

He nods. "That seems right."

He appears to be having trouble making eye contact with me, so I look away, too.

Then I turn back, struck with an idea. "I've got it! There's this scene in the first season of *Bridgerton* where Daphne and the duke are in the art gallery together.

Standing in front of some gorgeous painting and having an *experience* side by side."

"Yeah?" he asks, indifferently.

"Yes!" I say. "And their pinkies are almost touching. That was sexy." I contemplate it for a moment, remembering with a roll of desire in my low belly. "Just, because you could tell they were both so *aware* of each other, you know?"

He huffs out a very un-Easton-like—almost grim—laugh.

"Yeah, Hanna," he says. "I know."

Aaaaugh.

I need Hanna not to talk.

Specifically, I need her not to talk about masturbation or sex or when the last time she did either was.

Because it makes me *wonder* about things.

Like what she does when she's alone.

The curse of having known more than a few women intimately is knowing how much variety there is in how they pleasure themselves.

What's Hanna's method?

Teeny tiny bullet vibes delivering a buzzy charge straight to her clit?

On her belly, towel or pillow between her legs, rubbing while the pressure builds?

Or a hand slipped between her legs, teasing down her seam, finding herself wet, then moving back up to circle...?

Must. Stop.

In an effort to quit this madness, I drift over to where

Kane is standing with Mari, who has baby Zara in a sling on her belly. Amanda is already trying to suss out whether Zara is awake and whether she can hold her. Answer, no.

But Mari has to repeat the drill several times as the other family members join us. Everyone congratulates Kane on his success, tells him how much they love the photos—and asks for Z time.

"When she wakes up," Kane says firmly. He gazes down at Mari and Z with so much affection that it makes my chest hurt, which I tell myself is just because there has been so much damn monogamy happening around me lately.

"Oh, wow," Kane says, and we all turn to follow his glance.

The owner of the gallery has just slapped a red *sold* dot on a photo of Black Magic Canyon. Bear is standing in front of it, chatting with the owner. It's clear he's the one who bought it.

"Well, hell, that was decent of him," Kane says.

It was, which makes me feel a tiny bit... salty.

Amanda frowns at him. "Kane! He didn't do it to be nice. He did it because your photos kick ass."

"Yeah, yeah, yeah," Kane says.

He's definitely still trying to come to terms with his newfound talent and relative fame.

"But Bear *is* super nice."

We all turn to Hanna, who, unsurprisingly, is blushing again.

Lucy smiles at her. "Does that have anything to do with why I've never seen you wearing that top before?"

The top. Yes. I have some things to say about the top. It is blousy and red and scoop-necked, and this is now the third time I've seen this much of Hanna's breasts. Once again, it is a confusing but decidedly not unpleasant experience. She is so... generous and curvy and soft-looking and creamy and...

My mouth is *not* watering.

"Bear's been totally great," Hanna says, the blush deepening.

I scuff my shoe against the floor, irritated.

"He's obviously not local." Mari leans toward Hanna, her tone and expression gently razzing. "And he's not married or engaged."

"Nope," Rachel joins in. "Or if he is, it's the best kept secret on the Internet."

"So that means he's available," Jessa teases.

"Stop!" Hanna says. "You *guys*!"

She rolls her eyes, crosses her arms, and huffs off.

I watch her go. She's wearing a pair of snug-fitting jeans that have the definite privilege of cupping her ass.

Do. Not. Start. The. Underwear. Guessing. Game.

No lines...

Easton! I chide myself.

The gallery owner steps away from where he and Bear are standing in front of Kane's photograph, and Hanna sidles up to take his place.

She stands next to Bear, not looking at him. Their pinky fingers almost touch.

I close my eyes as tight as I can.

There are lots of things I could be feeling right now.

I could be laughing inside because Hanna is so adorably literal minded.

I could be flattered and pleased with myself because

Hanna took my suggestion that she do as Daphne would do.

I could be relieved that I successfully convinced Hanna that my knowledge of *Bridgerton* didn't extend beyond overhearing Amanda talking about it.

I could be thrilled for Hanna because Bear has just snuck a look in her direction—and then another slightly longer one.

Instead, I have an undefined twisted-up feeling somewhere in my chest or gut. Or both.

I tear my gaze away from them to find Amanda watching me.

Oh. No. That's bad. I school my face to neutrality.

"Sister dearest," Kane says to Amanda. "I don't hear any snarky commentary from you."

"Huh," she says. The corner of her mouth turns up in what I'd have to characterize as a smirk, and my stomach clenches a little more. "Rumor has it... Bear is Hanna's date tonight." She turns her gaze toward where Hanna and Bear are standing, and all the other eyes in our group follow.

Except mine; I choose not to look. Irritably, I shift from one foot to the other, watching them spy on our friends. Nothing stays secret in this family. It's ridiculous.

"Seriously?" Kane demands.

"Did she just *Bridgerton*-art-gallery-scene him?" Lucy demands.

"I think she did," Rachel says, amused.

"Wonder what *that's* all about," Amanda says.

Inexplicably, they all turn to me, eyebrows raised, like they're asking *me* for intel.

"What makes you think I know?" I shrug as nonchalantly as I can, while frustration rises in my chest like a river headed for flood stage.

I cross and uncross my arms while my family members' eyes search my face, as if the answer might be there.

When they're satisfied it isn't, their attention shifts back to Hanna.

And so does mine.

Those two pinky fingers are touching now.

And suddenly I just... can't. "I'd better..." I say.

I meant to say, "go," but I don't finish the sentence.

I turn away from them and stride toward the exit.

14

EASTON

The Monday morning after the photography exhibit, I meet with Bear.

Before Saturday, I'd been super excited about this meeting, because access to Bear is great on all counts. He can help me up my game on Wilder's social media channels and make me a better content producer. But spending time one-on-one with him will also help me argue—not in words, but in actions—that I'd be an asset to him as a partner.

But this morning, I drag ass to the meeting.

It's just...

It's just those two fucking pinkies, touching.

Or, really, it's my being an idiot about it.

As soon as I got out of that gallery and my head cleared, I felt foolish. So I've been having some confusing flashes of attraction for Hanna. So what? She's an attractive woman who's suddenly started wearing flattering clothes and makeup and generally putting herself out there as an available, sexual creature. Of *course* I'm going to notice.

But that's all there is to it.

It's just too absurd to imagine there being anything more.

Because then you get into scenarios like these, where I say to Hanna, "Hey. I've been spending a lot of time staring at your body lately, and I'm not so bearish on Bear. You should think about getting with me instead."

Uh, sure. *That's* going to fly.

I don't have a clear picture of how she'd respond. Probably, she would just burst out laughing and say something suitably deflating, along the lines of, "Ha!"

And then it's weird and awkward for a while, and my siblings notice and ask, and maybe Hanna even tells my sister and the others what happened...

Ugh. No.

Or...

Maybe Hanna says, "Huh! That sounds awesome," and we look at each other for a long time before I lean in, and she leans in...

I don't let myself imagine what happens next. I just skip ahead to where we get in a stupid spat about something, our friendship is ruined, and Gabe kills me in my sleep.

So, yeah.

Basically, I need to yank my head out of my ass, pull myself together. Probably get laid—

Britney?

I sigh, because it's like imagining eating spinach, for health.

Not like ice cream.

Not even pistachio ice cream.

"Easton?"

Bear is watching me with an amused expression, paused midway through explaining about the scheduling software he prefers.

"Sorry," I say, for what's starting to feel like the ten millionth time in the last couple weeks. "I'm with you now. Swear."

"I'm not boring you, am I?"

"Hell, no," I say. "No. I'm all in on this stuff. I just thought of something I need to... take care of."

I do my best to pay attention as Bear shows me how he plans his content schedule, how he decides when to reuse or repurpose footage across channels, and a bunch of other strategic stuff. It's absolute gold, and I lap it up.

"You're a quick study," he says, sounding pleased, when I suggest a way he could break up a long YouTube video and use it to create some TikToks. "And you've got such a good feel for the TikTok vibe."

"Thanks."

"But I should let you know. The more I think about it, the less I like the idea of the job being remote. I'm going to make it an on-site position."

On one hand that complicates things. Working for Bear would mean leaving not just Wilder Adventures, but also Rush Creek. But I'd also been thinking, since that conversation with my brothers in Oscar's, that maybe getting out of Rush Creek would have its benefits.

"You still want me to consider you?"

I hesitate only a split second. "Absolutely."

"Hey." His voice gets more serious. "About Hanna."

My stomach jolts, like the sickening drop of a roller coaster.

He doesn't quite make eye contact with me. "She's not... seeing anyone, is she? I just wanted to check to make sure I'm not treading on any toes if I spend more time with her."

I open my mouth. Close it again. "Uh, no," I say. "No. She's not seeing anyone."

"Not sure how to say this, but..." he hesitates.

Don't say it! I think. *If you're not sure how to, that means* don't say it at all!

People, in general, are way too hasty to get their feelings off their chests. Better, sometimes, to just hold back until you realize they're not actually all that interesting or important. Better to make a joke or just, you know, change the subject to something else entirely.

"You and she don't have anything going on, do you? You guys just seem to have a thing. A... flirty vibe."

I force a laugh. "Hanna and me? Definitely not. We've known each other since we were five. We don't see each other like that. Plus, we work together—I mean, all day, every day, year round, not like on a few workshops—" Okay, definitely babbling. "—it would be weird. So, no. No... *thing.*"

Bear blows a breath. "Oh, good," he says. "I, you know, didn't want to ruffle feathers."

"No feathers here," I say.

It is definitely time for me to stop talking.

"Thanks, man." Bear nods. "Appreciate it."

"Yeah. Any time."

We're both silent for a moment, and then Bear says, "Oh, let's talk about the Instagram algorithm and reels."

We shift gears and do just that, but my mind is still shifty, tripping back to the conversation we just finished. The one where everything I said was true, and yet... not quite.

15

———

HANNA

I swear to God I didn't sabotage Bear's truck, but I have to admit, the fact that he's staring forlornly at a flat feels like a gift from the universe.

"Want some help with that?" I ask.

His eyes come up. "Oh, hey, Hanna," he says, and beams at me. Which is really freaking gratifying. "I can change it, no prob." Of course he can; he's Bear Warden! "But I'm five minutes late for an appointment in town. Do you think you could drop me at the Depot Hotel? I can get a ride back here afterwards."

"Absolutely," I say.

"Nice truck," he says, climbing up. "I have a special place in my heart for a woman who drives a pickup."

I can feel myself blushing as I start the engine, then back out. Not all guys feel that way, I can tell you that. I think there's something to that whole thing about how guys are compensating for size anxiety with their trucks... but Bear seems chill... which is maybe because he doesn't have any compensating to do.

I guess you could say I have a special place in my heart for guys who have special places in their hearts for women who drive pickups.

Bear takes up a lot of space in my truck, which makes it feel small for the first time in its history. Also, he smells like wool and cookstove oil and the end of a long day at the office, which is…

Not as awesome as you might think.

But probably just temporary. I am 100 percent sure he's going to take a long hot shower and use obscene amounts of Irish Spring, Prell, and Old Spice.

"Hey, Han?" he asks, as we pull onto the road to town.

I like that he's picked up my friends' nickname for me. "Yeah?"

"I have a… question for you."

"A… question?"

I don't mean to mimic his words, but the seriousness in his voice has hijacked the word part of my brain, like when I was in middle school and a boy tried to talk to me.

Come to think of it, not much has changed. Still totally deer in the headlights.

Easton and I *so* should have practiced this. I'm fine when I don't like the guy in question, but as soon as the stakes go up, I freeze.

I make a note: Practice all things that might come up and require a semi-smooth, semi-human response from me, vis-a-vis Bear and dating.

"I was hoping maybe we could get to know each other a little better. Spend some time together—in and out of the woods."

There's the can't-breathe, heart-kicking-up sensation. *In and out of the woods* sounds deliciously sexy.

"I—I'd like that."

"Aw, good," he says. "I was kinda hoping. How would you feel about dinner Saturday night?"

"I'd feel good about that."

He nods. "There's this place in Bend that specializes in forage and farm-to-table."

"That sounds... amazing."

I roll my eyes, internally, at myself. Apparently, no matter how down to earth you *think* you are, the right guy can still ruin your vocabulary.

"Great!" Bear says buoyantly. "Cypress can get some footage ahead of time so they can focus on just filming us on Saturday."

Whoa. What? "Filming... us...?"

"Oh, shit," Bear says. "I wasn't thinking. I should have asked first. Are you okay with Cypress documenting it?"

"Documenting it?"

"It goes with the territory with me, unfortunately," he says. "I mean, not all the time, but I do end up living certain aspects of my life in public. In this case, I was thinking it would make sense, because my viewers *really* like you, and they're shipping us."

"Shipping? Us?"

I'm really just helplessly repeating his words, not trying to question the premise, but it sounds a little like I'm doubting the possibility of what he's saying.

"You know, wanting us to be together."

"Yeah, I know what shipping is, I just—"

I still don't have words.

"I guess I was just hoping we could give my viewers a little window on our first date. Not much. Just a few video clips of us enjoying each other's company."

Our *first* date.

Kinda loving that, especially the implication that he's already thinking about more than one.

But dating on camera?

Huh.

"I don't know," I say slowly. I mean, I get it. It *does* go with the territory if you're someone like Bear Warden, especially if you're Bear Warden going on a date with someone his viewers already know and like.

"I don't want you to feel pressured into it. I know it makes some women nervous. But you seem so comfortable with yourself, and with the cameras. And you're very beautiful. You must know that."

"I. Uh. Thank you."

I spend a second or two trying to figure out how I feel about this *beautiful,* noting that for some reason it doesn't pack the same punch as *pretty*.

But he thinks I'm beautiful. Which, win!! So yeah. I let myself revel in that.

"If there's anything you want to cut afterwards, anything that feels too personal, you can always tell me. No questions asked."

I want to say, *What about kissing? Will Cypress film us* kissing?

Because I'm running a film montage in my head: Bear, hugging me as I arrive at the restaurant, pulling out my chair for me as we both laugh at something witty I've said, reaching across the table to hold my hand, pouring a little more wine into my glass. Leaning in and touching his plush lips to mine.

We look good together. I'm beautiful. And his viewers *love* us.

That doesn't suck.

"Cypress can film," I tell him. "As long as you promise to cut any clip where I trip all over myself like a dope."

For some reason, an imaginary version of Easton interjects, *No fucking way. Those are the best parts.* I swallow a snicker.

"I just can't imagine you doing anything like a dope," Bear says, his voice warm.

Aw.

Also, he doesn't know me very well yet.

Town comes into view. Rush Creek has a strong Western feel—low slung buildings with long plank siding, bright-colored doors, and shutters. At some point during the transformation from rodeo town to girls' getaway, the chamber of commerce installed flower baskets and Craftsman-style faux gas lamps everywhere, giving all of Rush Creek the feel of a made-for-TV small-town movie.

I turn from South Street onto Main Street, past Rush to Read Books, Morning Rush Coffee, and Rush Creek Bakery. Like most Rush Creek denizens, I'm nostalgic for the rodeo days... but I have to admit, I admire how the town has adapted to its new identity.

I pull up in front of the Depot Hotel, with its aggressively Western-styled front porch.

"Text me your address and I'll pick you up at 6:15 on Saturday," he says. "I'll be looking forward to it."

By the time I can ponder whether "nervously anticipating, with some doubts" counts as "looking forward to," and therefore whether I can truthfully say, "me too," he's out of the truck and gone.

16

"Wait," I say. "I don't understand."

Hanna shrugs. "There's nothing *to* understand."

"No, I think there's *a lot* to understand. He asks you on a date, and he also says his viewers are shipping you guys and he wants to—" I crook my fingers hard into air quotes—"give them a window. Is he asking you out? Or is he asking you to act a part? And why is this not making *your* head spin?"

We're the last two people at Wilder HQ tonight, because we told Bear we'd pull the group gear together for the next workshop.

Hanna has just filled me on Bear's invitation to her, and I'm...

Pissed.

"I really don't get what your beef is, E. He *was* clear. He was very straightforward. He said I'm beautiful. That he wanted to get to know me better."

I can't see her face because she's digging in one of the

big plastic storage totes, looking for a lightweight pot. But I don't have to look at her to tell she's blushing fiercely. I can hear it in the way she says the word beautiful, and it makes me want to yank the entire tote out of her hands, force her to look at me, and tell her exactly what I think of Bear's plan to film their date. To turn a special night with Hanna into a spectacle.

Hanna is zero bullshit. You don't come at her with… with *this*.

"Does Gabe know?" I demand.

"I gave him a heads up that I was going out with Bear." She unfolds herself from the container, triumphant, holding the pot aloft. "He said as long as it was fine with me, it wasn't his business, since Bear's not an employee. And," she shrugs, "he said that it would probably be good publicity for Wilder."

"Okay, *how is that fair*?" I howl. "When I flirt on trips, it's a distraction. When you flirt on trips, it's a business plan."

"What is *wrong* with you?" Hanna demands. With more force than necessary, she shoves the pot into a duffel. "This has nothing to do with me flirting or anything. This is about Bear being interested in me and wanting to *explore* things."

I *hate* the word explore. I hate it with the power of a thousand fiery suns. I especially hate the way Hanna just said it, dripping with suggestion, conjuring up images of Hanna and Bear doing dirty deeds in their shared tent in the woods.

"He's *using you*," I burst out, before I can think better of it.

Hanna's mouth flattens, and I instantly regret my words.

Because deep down, I know I'm being a complete, irrational, asshole. What Bear has proposed is a little... unconventional... but in truth, I think his intentions are probably mostly pure. He just wants to get to know Hanna better—and his life happens to be carried out in the spotlight.

I think the likelihood is high that he has feelings for Hanna and wants to follow them to their logical conclusion.

And I just totally and completely rained on Hanna's parade because—

"You're just jealous." She accuses me, then folds her arms and stares me down—and I can't take it. I look away, the accusation settling like in my gut like...

Like the truth.

This is it. I can deny it like my life depends on it, or I can look her straight in the eye and admit that she's right.

I think about when I was out with my brothers at Oscar's and we were talking about whether I've been picking the "wrong" women. I'd told them I didn't think there was a *right* woman for me, that I'd never felt like there was something or someone out there that I needed but couldn't find.

It was the truth. But maybe only a partial truth. And right now, finally, I admit to myself that the other half of the truth has been trying to get my attention for days. Ever since Bear Warden walked into the Wilder offices and Hanna Hott blushed.

There isn't something *out there* that I need but can't find.

There's something closer to home that I didn't know I wanted until it was...

Jesus. Until it was too late.

I take a deep breath. "You're ri—"

Hanna smacks a hand onto the flat plastic top of one of the totes. "You're jealous because Bear wants to put *me* on camera, and he hasn't said word one to you about putting *you* on camera. And you're the one who wants the job from him."

My mouth is still open, the words caught in my throat.

"I know you want this job, Easton. I totally get it. But I want this *guy*."

Her voice pleads with me.

Hanna is pleading.

And what kind of selfish asshole takes this long to figure his shit out, and then jumps in and wrecks things for two good people?

Not me.

I take a deep breath.

I get my head on straight.

"You're right, Han. I was being a dick. I'm sorry."

"Good," she says. "Glad you know it. Because I need your help with something."

I pause with a Ziploc bag of oats in my hands. "Sure," I say. "What do you need my help with?"

She probably wants to know what I think she should wear. Or maybe whether I think she should let him pay or offer to split the check.

"Kissing practice," she says.

17

______

HANNA

The look on Easton's face is comical.

"Oh, come on," I tell him. "I'd do it for you." I think about that a moment. "I mean, if you didn't have the equivalent of ten thousand hours of kissing practice and actually *needed* help."

He opens his mouth, as if to protest, but I need him to understand this. "This is the big leagues, Easton. This is Bear Warden, he's basically my perfect guy, and I'm on *fucking* camera, on the fucking Internet. It's hard enough being on camera, period, without running the risk that there will be a viral video of me closing my eyes, leaning in, and looking like a frog."

He crosses his arms. "You won't look like a frog," he says.

"How do you *know*? This is why I need your help. It's one thing to kiss a guy for the first time on your front stoop or in the privacy of the backseat of his car. Or on the hood of his car in the parking lot behind Oscar's—"

"Oh, God, Hanna, stop!" he says, closing his eyes and ducking his head like I've hurt him.

"I'm just saying that this isn't just a first date. It's a public first date."

"Right," he grumbles. "This is why I was saying that's a terrible fucking ide—"

I show him my open palm. "Not rehashing that. You said your piece, you apologized, and now you're doing penance."

"In the form of kissing practice," he says.

I sigh. "If the idea of kissing me is that loathsome—"

"No," he interrupts, startling me. "I didn't say that. I didn't fucking say that." He rakes his hand through his hair. "It's just—I think it's a bad idea. Friends smushing their faces together."

"Aw," I say.

"What?"

"I just like it when you say we're friends."

He buries his head in both hands.

"Fine. Fine. I won't mention the fact that we're friends again. But I will remind you that Gabe would be extremely interested in the fact that you're trying to convince Bear Warden to give you a job."

He closes his eyes. Tight. "You are... incorrigible."

The thing is, I don't think that word means what he thinks it does, because he sounds actually a little...

Fond.

He sounds fond of me.

And when he opens his eyes again, they are soft on my face. Affectionate.

I like it. A little too much.

But I'm also not above using it to my advantage.

"Easton," I say. "You said it yourself. We're friends. Friends help each other out. I've been losing sleep thinking about doing this kissing thing on camera. You don't want me to lose more sleep! Or, worse, humiliate myself publicly."

"You will *not* humiliate yourself publicly."

"I might! You think kissing is the kind of everyday event no one can screw up, like tying your shoes or riding a bike or blowing your nose."

"I do *not* think kissing is like blowing your nose," Easton says, clearly offended.

"I just mean in terms of frequency."

He starts to say something, then stops.

We've both abandoned the gear-gathering. The totes are open around us, the duffel slouched and unzipped. I set down the plastic lid I'm holding and tell him, "For me, kissing is more like... hang-gliding."

He tilts his head in question.

"Rare and terrifying every time," I clarify.

He rakes his hand through his hair again. It's standing on end from all the abuse. "Hanna," he begins, then stops. He paces a few steps away from me, a few back. When his eyes meet mine, there's something a little frantic in them. "Kissing *should* be like hang-gliding. All kissing should be like hang-gliding. And if it starts being like nose-blowing, then you're definitely doing it wrong."

"See?!" I exclaim. "This is exactly why you're the right guy for this job. You are a kissing guru. A kissing virtuoso. I need the master."

"You're killing me," he pleads.

"No," I correct. "Gabe is going to kill you, if he finds out you're looking for a new job."

Something flares in Easton's eyes. He crosses his arms. "Let's get something straight." His voice is rough. "You don't have to bribe me to kiss you. I don't want you thinking that. That this is some hardship. That kissing you is something you have to extort from me with bribes or threats, that that's the only way I'd want to—" Another pass of his long, thick fingers through his beautiful, rumpled hair.

"I'm happy to do it, Hanna. Anyone should be happy to do it. Lucky to do it—"

Blood has suddenly rushed to parts of my body I didn't think were having this conversation with Easton. It's the way he says "happy" and "lucky," the way he's looking at me right now—

Like he means it. Like he wants to do it. Not just because he wants to be a friend, or help me, but because he wants...

Because he wants *me*.

But then he turns away, his shoulders giving a little shudder or shake.

Silly Hanna! This is Easton Wilder, king of pussy. He can have anyone he wants, any time he wants.

Besides, *I* don't want Easton to want me. I want *Bear* to want me.

I inform my constricted lungs and overworking heart that they can chill the fuck out now, because we're returning to planet earth.

When Easton turns back to me, his face is neutral, and whatever heat I thought I saw in his eyes is gone. He gives a slight, tight nod.

When he speaks again, the rough, impassioned note is gone from his voice, and he just sounds... tired.

"And we're friends. So, if this is what you need to feel comfortable on this... date... thing... I will help you out."

18

———

EASTON

God help me.

God fucking help me.

Actually, I think I'm past that. I think the moment for help passed right around the moment that I agreed to help Hanna shop for new clothes, or maybe the moment when I saw her pinky finger touch Bear's in the art gallery, or... well, it's officially gone.

I loathe myself for agreeing to this, but I seem to have lost the ability to say no to Hanna, and also...

And also, I want to.

God help me, I want to.

From the tips of my toes to my suddenly dry mouth and all the parts in between, including the one that flushed thick with blood when she presented me with the image of her getting kissed over the hood of a car.

(By me. I substituted myself into that frame, without a second thought.)

Hanna is watching me with a very Hanna-like look on

her face. She looks curious, as if people—as if I—don't *quite* make sense to her, and she's struggling to connect the dots.

Good luck, Hanna, because these days I don't make sense to myself, either.

"Okay," she says slowly. "So. How do we do this?"

I look around at our surroundings, at the open storage totes and the camping supplies. "Not here," I say. "For one thing, Gabe or Lucy could come running over at any moment to grab something they forgot. Or any one of my family members could show up."

And I would never, ever be able to explain this. I can't even explain it to myself. Plus, if Hanna gets caught kissing me, it will put her in a really awkward position when she goes viral kissing Bear.

Hanna deserves to be kissed—even for practice—somewhere better than this. Somewhere private, somewhere quiet, somewhere where she can relax completely and just enjoy herself.

Scratch that. I need not to think about Hanna enjoying herself.

I grab a tote lid and jam it back on its mate. "Let's go to my place. I've got a bottle of wine—you might as well make this as realistic as possible, because if he kisses you on the first date, you're going to have a glass or two in you."

She nods. "My lips get all numb and tingly when I drink."

There goes the wild flush of blood to my cock. There goes that sensation, almost like hunger, of wanting to trap her mouth with mine and lick those tingles into flame.

I never want her to tell Bear that thing about her lips. I don't want her to say any of the things in her head, the things that roll off her tongue with so little filter, that make my blood boil, to him.

He's basically my perfect guy, she said.

Bear. Is. What. Hanna. Wants.

I'm too late, and the best I can do now is to be the friend she deserves.

"Let's clean this shit up and go get you up to speed on kissing," I say.

WE PARK Hanna's truck and my Jeep in the parking lot of my townhouse complex.

I'm nervous, which shouldn't be the case. I have never gotten nervous about kissing someone. I'm supposed to be the expert in this scenario.

I remind myself that I don't have to impress her. All I have to do is allow my lips to be exploited for Hanna's self-growth.

This is not a test.

She stands back so I can unlock the door and let her in.

"This is nice," she says, stepping inside.

"Wait, you've never been here?"

She shrugs. "I mean, no?"

I try to see it through her eyes. It's a two-bedroom townhouse in one of the nicer complexes in Rush Creek. It used to be mostly live-in owners, but since Rush Creek got fancified, a lot of the apartments have been turned over to vacation rentals. We're standing in the foyer staring at the backside of a flight of stairs, the great room behind them and the kitchen on my right. It's well lit, with big windows and skylights, and back in the day when bringing a woman back to my condo was my sole goal in life, I hired a decorator to make it cozy and welcoming.

Today, through Hanna's eyes, it's kind of... impersonal. There's nothing within sight that says anything about who I am or what I care about. And for the first time, that *bothers* me.

"I want to redecorate," I say, meaning it, though I've never had that thought before. I lead her into the great room and gesture to the sofa, where she plops down and leans back into the pillows. Her breasts jiggle appealingly as she lands, and for a moment, all I want is to follow her down, start the kissing practice right this fucking second— but I know that impulse comes from nowhere good. *She's Bear's,* I remind myself.

It doesn't get any better with repetition.

"Yeah?" she says. "What would you do if you redecorated?"

I think about it a moment. "Kane took a ton of photos of me working on my kayak. Different stages."

"On your kayak?" she asks.

"Yeah, you know, the one I'm building?"

"I didn't know you were building a kayak."

"Yeah," I say. "It's from a kit, but—"

"That's so cool!"

My chest warms. "I could, you know, show you some time."

"Yeah. I want to see. Why don't you ever talk about it?"

I shrug. "Dunno. Never seemed like the right moment."

She frowns at me. "You mean because someone else is always talking. It can be hard to get a word in edgewise in that crew." For a moment her eyes, cool and blue, linger on my face, her lashes long, thick, and black. Then it's her turn to shrug. "I get why making jokes and charming the shit out of everyone is your best strategy."

"You think that's what I do."

She rolls her eyes. "Easton. Come on."

"It's not a *strategy*."

"No," she says. "More like a defense mechanism."

Startled, I look at her, and she looks back. Her expression is un-Hanna-like, soft and sympathetic. And I discover that I can't actually *talk*. Because I think she might be right.

"Where's that wine you promised me?" she demands, saving me from my sudden inability to form words.

"Uh, hang on."

I head for the kitchen. "What do you like?" I call.

"Red," she says.

"Can you be more specific?"

"No."

I laugh and liberate an unopened bottle of French Malbec from my wine rack. I'd let myself forget for a moment why we're here, but pouring wine into glasses reminds me, and my pulse kicks back up. I carry the glasses into the living room and hand her one. She's not dressed in any of her new clothes right now, just a pair of hiking pants and a t-shirt that bares her round arms and the pale upper curves of her glorious tits.

I sit down next to her. "So," I say. "How are you thinking this whole thing goes down?"

She gets a faraway look in her eyes. "He's picking me up, so I'm assuming we get this fancy pants dinner, and, I don't know? Lots of flirting at the table, right? Like, I lick a drop of wine off the rim of my glass and look up at him through my lashes?"

"That's so *calculating*!" I say, admiringly, also a little bit stuck on the image of Hanna licking a drop of wine off... well, anything... and wishing she'd do it now, to demonstrate. Should I ask?

I could ask. *Show me how you do that. With the wine licking.*

"Do you honestly think we all just do that? Accidentally?" she demands. "Or we're just so overcome by your sexiness that we can't help licking things, randomly?"

"I mean, no, but—"

"Oh, I get it. You just didn't think *I* knew how to do that stuff," she accuses.

"I—I guess I thought you were too honest to."

She rolls her eyes. "It has nothing to do with honesty and everything to do with using what you've got."

My eyes drop for the briefest second to her mouth, plump and red and a little shiny from the sip of wine she just took.

"And then... I don't know! You tell me. Does he make a move on me when we walk back to the car? When we get in the car? Or not until he drops me back at my house?"

I try to put myself in Bear's shoes. Sitting across from her, joking with her, that smart mouth and quick mind, the way she's always there with an observation off the beaten track. Not like anyone else. And she'll be wearing something from her new wardrobe, maybe, with a deeper scoop even than the shirt she's wearing now, and he'll have been trying to keep his eyes off the soft white satin of her skin for hours, wondering what it would feel like against his lips, and...

And the *licking*.

I cough. "Okay, so, thinking cinematically," I say. "Either when you walk back to the car or when he drops you off. Because in the car is just a beast to film."

"Right," she says, with a sigh. "So do you think it's safe to say when he drops me off?"

"Probably," I agree. "Unless your granddad's sitting on the porch, and then all bets are off."

"Oh, *God*," she says. "I'll get Aunt Meryl to take Granddad to Bingo or something for the evening. Or make him promise not to commit violence of any kind, at least."

"Okay, so let's assume you can remove him from the scene. Bear drops you off and comes around the car to open your door. Give him time to do that!" I instruct.

"Got it. So, he's waiting for me to get out, and I stand up..."

"Right." I stand up, move so I'm closer to where Hanna is sitting. "You're going to stand up, and when you do, depending on whether he steps back or not..."

She wriggles across the couch as if she were sliding out of a car seat, and that wriggle stirs something animal and ravenous in my gut. Then she's standing, so close to me that her scent fills me up. This close, she smells like a garden, like a thousand species of flowers all rioting for summer. And I can feel the heat of her body and the brush of her clothing, and a fierce tug of sheer, sharp *want*. I don't even have to think about what would happen next; I don't have to plan or calculate; I just bend down and cup my hand behind the silky curve of her head and drop my mouth to hers.

Which is soft, even softer than it looks, and warm. When our lips touch, she exhales a tiny, almost-surprised breath, and her hands come up and grip my arms, tight. I groan, my free hand dropping to her waist, her hip, slipping around to find the soft curve of her ass, tugging her hard up against me. I open my mouth over hers, and hers opens in instant welcome. I delve in, trying to sate the hunger that's been building in me, trying to get more of her, enough of her, but it turns out there isn't enough of her, no matter how close I tug her, how tight I pull her against me, how perfect her tongue feels teasing mine. I want more, more, more...

I break away, panting.

She's panting too, her chest heaving—I try not to stare but holy mother of God she's pretty like this, all want and breathless need, and I want to kiss her again and make her pant and beg and plead for more.

I wipe my mouth with the back of my hand, I wipe my forehead with the front of my hand, I close my eyes and press my face into both my palms.

"I—" I start.

Everything I want to say collects like gathering storm clouds at the back of my throat, stuck there, and in the end, all I can say is,

"I can't do this."

19

———————

HANNA

Bear takes me, as promised, to this amazing farm-to-table restaurant in Bend, called Luminous. We're seated at a table for two next to a window that looks out at the mountains. The table is covered with a white linen tablecloth, and two real candles flicker as the server places big thick-paper menus in front of us, which he assures us are updated daily with new items.

Bear's assistant has set up shop a little distance away, surprisingly inconspicuous, but we're mic'd and I can tell that Cypress is capturing our every move on camera.

"What looks good to you?" Bear asks me.

"It all looks amazing," I say. "I'm leaning towards the halibut and the smoked salmon appetizer, the one with creme fraiche on cornmeal—how do you say this? Rillettes? Yum."

"Would you want to split that?"

No! I think. *I want it all!* "Sure," I say.

Easton wouldn't have asked me that. He knows I don't like to share my food.

Which is a completely ridiculous thought. Easton and I wouldn't be at Luminous, eating forty-five-dollar entrees.

But if we were, he would know better than to ask me to share.

Damn it, I wish I hadn't thought about Easton. Because now another thought is trying to slip in the door.

Or not a thought exactly.

A full-on sense memory.

The feel of Easton's body before I even touched it, when I stood up closer to him than I meant to, still thinking that we were just *practicing*. There were a couple of inches between us, but those inches didn't exist in that moment, because I could feel the heat of his skin, the deliciousness of chemical energy jumping the gap between us, tugging us together. It was a shock... and also not, because it felt so familiar that it was more like a homecoming.

And then his mouth—

"We'll split the smoked salmon appetizer," Bear is saying to the server, who has materialized during my mental absence.

Shit. I'm *not* supposed to be thinking about Easton and our *practice kiss* right now.

I'm not supposed to think about that kiss at all, because it wasn't a real kiss. It was just a...

Just a...

His mouth.

It's not news that Easton Wilder has a beautiful mouth, slightly too wide, with surprisingly full lips for a man. I have occasionally admired it, the way I can admire art in a museum or a car I'll never have the money to buy.

But now I've kissed that mouth, and I can attest: He knows how to use it.

Commanding.

Fierce.

Hungry.

That tongue, too. So skilled, the way it teased my lower lip and stroked my tongue, setting me on fire so I found myself kissing back in ways I hadn't even thought about before—avidly, hungrily, messily, but also *sweetly*, like I just wanted to show him something that I hadn't been able to find any words for before.

He was showing me something, too, and I wanted to know more about it, I wanted to sink into the couch and pull him down on top of me so he could show me everything he meant, everything he was trying to say.

Except of course, he absolutely wasn't. That part was just my fantasy.

He made that absolutely clear when he said, "I can't do this."

"Hanna?" Bear says, and I get the feeling it's not the first time he's said it. "Did you want to order your entree?"

"Shit, sorry—I don't know where my head was—yes, I'll have the halibut," I tell the server, and he smiles and writes it down, so it can't have been too too long that I was sitting there like a fool, dreaming about a mouth that was just mine for *practice*.

THE DATE PLAYS out more or less the way Easton and I predicted. Although I don't lick wine off the rim of my glass, and there's not much flirting. I'm just not in the mood for it, and Bear's a good conversationalist, but everything he says is so earnest. He lectures me on the importance of farm-to-table cuisine—which, don't get me wrong, I totally agree with, where it's possible. And he asks a *lot* of questions about my childhood and doesn't seem to get the message that I hate talking about myself. I keep changing the subject back to him—and every time I do, he seems perfectly happy to launch into another lecture—on spring greens or late summer nuts or trapping rabbits. I successfully deflect and deflect and deflect from my own story and try to look rapt and fascinated while he's educating me.

Then he talks for a *loooong* time about this foraging-and-cooking competition he's going to enter next fall and how he's pretty sure he's a shoe-in. He seems to want reassurance, so I tell him of course he's going to do great, and he laps that up while Cypress gets in close on the shot.

It's fine, don't get me wrong, it's just—

I guess I find myself wishing for him to take things a little less seriously, to take me a little less seriously, and above all, to take himself a little less seriously.

He could learn a lesson or two from—

No.

Stop.

Bear picks up the check—he insists, and Cypress zooms in again to capture our slight tussle on camera, which... well, whatever, it's fine. Bear's rich and famous and I'm *Hanna,* and it doesn't make sense for me to fight him on this. Besides, I'm the one who thought it might not be so bad to be treated, just for a little while, like a princess.

Spoiler: It's not *so* bad.

He doesn't make a move in the Luminous parking lot, but on the drive back to my granddad's place, I start to get massively nervous, because I'm pretty sure he's going to do exactly what Easton and I predicted and go in for a kiss when I get out of the car. And I can't figure out how I feel about that anymore.

Which sucks, because before the kissing practice, everything seemed so *simple*.

I want to rewind to before Easton touched his mouth to mine.

Except I don't. Not really.

I want to rewind and then *relive* it a few more thousand times.

Which worries me even more.

Bear pulls his truck up in front of my granddad's house. He gets out, and I wait for him to do exactly what Easton mapped out, to come gallantly around to open my door.

He's taking a long time, so long that I get impatient, and then I realize what's happening:

He's giving Cypress enough time to set up a shot on us.

Right. OK. That's OK. This was always part of the plan. I practiced so I wouldn't look like a frog.

Practicing makes me think about Easton again, which is...

Not what I should be thinking about as Bear (finally) comes around and opens my door.

He steps back as I slide down, taking my hand. And then he very gently tugs me toward him. "Hanna," he murmurs, leaning close. "I had a really good time tonight."

"Me too." I mean, it's not *far* from the truth. The food was out of this world. I don't get many chances to eat food

like that. And I still find Bear incredibly physically attractive and compelling, and I'm looking forward to this kiss.

Bear locks his eyes on mine.

His eyes are very blue, but they don't...

They don't make me...

They don't make me feel like a molten pool of me.

Hanna! I chide myself.

This man *wants* me. He thinks I'm beautiful. He's here,
with me, and this night is *not* going to end with him saying,
I can't do this.

Right. I look up at his handsome face.

It's sort of *looming*. Like we're in super slow-mo. And his
breath as it brushes across my skin is... winey. And smells
like the steak he ate.

I mean, not awful or anything.

And then Bear leans in and kisses me and it's...

It's okay.

20

———

EASTON

"E? You okay?" Brody asks.

He and I are sitting at the bar at Oscar's, nursing a couple of single malt scotches. He called me up about an hour ago, told me that Rachel was hosting a party and Justin was with his mom, and asked if I wanted to pay too much for quality booze.

I said yes, if only so I could stop wearing out the carpet in my living room, pacing.

I've known Brody's question was coming all evening, because try as I might, I can't pretend I'm my normal, happy-go-lucky self. I mean, I'm not sulking, either, but I'm —distracted. I keep checking the time, trying to figure out where Hanna is. Still at the restaurant with Bear? Finishing up and fighting over the check? Because of course she would—no way she's just going to let Bear pay. She's going to try to grab the check right out of his hand.

Despite my dark mood, it makes me smile to think about that.

I hope she wins that fight.

By now, though, they have to be at Hanna's house, right? It's after ten. I've started checking my phone more often, hoping against hope that I'll get a text from her.

Even though the way we left things really wasn't great.

I can't do this.

Hanna's face, a little hurt, a lot confused. *Okay?*

You should probably go.

Mainly because I was afraid if she didn't, I'd tell her I wanted to kiss her again, I wanted her to end things with Bear, I wanted her to be mine… and that would make me the worst kind of selfish dick.

Okay?

I haven't heard from her or texted her since because I'm afraid of what happens next. Afraid if she asks me to explain myself, I will, and then I'll be the asshole I've been trying not to be.

"*Easton?*"

Brody is just plain exasperated with me now.

"Sorry. Sorry."

"No," Brody says flatly. "Sorry isn't gonna cut it. What the fuck is going on with you? It's like you're not here at all. You've checked your phone, what, a hundred times in the last hour."

"I'm—"

"Don't apologize again!" Brody yelps.

I'd been about to, but I press my lips together.

Brody crosses his arms. "Does this have anything to do with Hanna's date?"

"Hanna's date?" I bluster. I didn't realize anyone besides Gabe and me even knew a date was in the offing.

"Yeah, Hanna's date with Bear. Rachel told me they were going out tonight. I guess Lucy found out from Gabe and told Rach. Just wondering if your mood has something to do with that?"

"No! Why would it?"

Brody's eyebrows go up. He doesn't say anything, just spears me with a look.

I crumble. Drop my elbows onto the bar and my head into my hands. Mutter, "I'm so fucked."

"You want to tell me what's going on?" Brody asks.

Without raising my head, I say, "I wish I knew."

"I think you do, East."

"It doesn't make any *sense*."

"This shit never does," Brody says mildly. "Just tell me. I'm not going to—whatever you're afraid of. Laugh. Judge you. Tell Gabe."

Unwillingly, I raise my head to find Brody's sympathetic eyes on me. "Don't," I say.

"What?"

"I don't want your pity."

Brody snorts. "Whatever, man. I don't *pity* you. I just know what it's like to want someone you *think* you can't have."

I don't ask Brody how he sussed me out. For a guy who's let people pin the bad boy label on him for most of his life, he's actually very soft-hearted and sensitive. That's probably why, of all my brothers, he's the one I'd fess up to first in a pinch.

Which is what I'm in now. A pinch. Of my own making.

But it's still hard to say it out loud. To admit to him what I've just barely been able to admit to myself.

"She asked me to—"

Am I really going to tell him this?

"She asked me to practice kissing with her."

Brody's eyes get huge. "No *way*. And?"

"And," I say, nodding. "And, and, *and*. You know how you asked me if it was possible that I've been having sex with the wrong people?"

A slow smile forms on Brody's face. "That's great, East!"

I shake my head. Hard. "No. It *sucks*. Because she's *Hanna*."

"What's that supposed to mean?"

"It means she's my friend. It means I work with her. It means that it's complicated and messy and Gabe would stuff an apple in my mouth, roast my head, and serve it on a silver platter."

Brody winces. "Colorful." He tilts his head. "Okay. Yes. I see your point. I guess it depends on what you want out of it… and what she wants out of it. If you're on the same page, maybe it doesn't have to be messy?"

"It's *always* messy," I say grimly. "Someone always wants more. Someone always gets their feelings hurt."

"But like you said, she's *Hanna*," Brody says. "If there's anyone in the world who knows what she wants, will be honest about it, and won't bullshit herself or anyone else, it's her, right?"

"I can guarantee you she doesn't want anything out of it except kissing practice. She's got such a lady boner for Bear, you wouldn't even believe it."

"Maybe. Or maybe you just haven't asked the right questions yet."

I frown at him. "What do you mean?"

"Maybe she also liked the kissing more than she expected to. In my humble experience, it takes two to tango, most of the time. Did she seem into it?"

For the first time since I kissed her, I let myself remember it. *Really* remember it. That gasp of surprise, her hands clutching my arms, the way she opened to me.

Her breath, fast and chaotic, and the flush on her cheeks and the *want* in her eyes.

She was so fucking hot.

I wanted her so bad.

And... I think... she wanted me.

"She seemed into it," I acknowledge. "But Gabe—"

Brody scowls. "You're just making excuses, E. And you know why I think that is? Because you're not used to wanting someone and not knowing if they want you back. You're used to always knowing *exactly* where you stand. But if you're not just going to keep having vanilla ice cream sex, you're going to have to take a chance."

He's right about that; I can't deny it.

"So, what, I just...?"

"Just find a time when the two of you are alone and lay it on her. *Hanna, I know we were just practicing, but...*

"I want to screw your brains out?" I grimace.

Brody frowns. "I'm sure the Wilder master of charm can find a more diplomatic way to put it."

He makes it sound so easy.

I hide my face, and my thoughts, by taking another slug of beer.

"Honesty's the best policy, E."

Is it?

Because if honesty were actually the best policy, I would also have told him that I'm trying to get hired by Bear and leave Wilder Adventures—and my brothers—behind.

21

HANNA

"We're making you brunch," Amanda declares.

My girlfriends have just shown up on my front porch in a giant posse, arms full. A waffle iron, bags of fruit, grocery bags stuffed, I assume, with ingredients.

I cross my arms. "Oh, come *on*," I say. "You want to pick my brain, and you know food is the best way to soften me up. You know if you showed up here empty handed and tried to get the dirt, I'd kick you out without ceremony."

Amanda and Rachel exchange looks. "There may be some truth to that," Amanda admits. "Waffles with berries, bananas, whipped cream, dark chocolate sauce, and mini marshmallows?"

As much as I don't want to talk about it—any of it—I'm ravenous and a total sucker for brunch food. Amanda knows me.

I hold the door open wide enough for Amanda and her minions to pass through. Amanda, Rachel, Lucy, Jessa,

Mari (Zara asleep in the sling on her chest), and Jessa's bestie and business partner, Imani. They tromp into the kitchen, set their bribes on the kitchen counters, and get immediately to work.

"What's all this?" my grandfather harumphs, shuffling into the kitchen.

"Hello, Mr. Hott," Amanda says, and the other women echo her. My grandfather doesn't bother to respond to the greetings, just repeats his question.

Amanda delivers her food porn litany.

My grandfather crosses his arms. "Is there enough for me?"

"Of course!" Amanda says. "And thank you for the party invitations!"

Thanks mostly to Aunt Meryl, invitations to my grand-dad's eighty-fifth are out, and RSVP cards have started appearing in our mailbox. Every day there's a new bunch, and my grandfather combs through them, growling when he doesn't find what he wants. I know what he's looking for —responses from my brothers.

I want to tell him it's not going to happen, but I know he won't listen. He'll keep up his hopeful march down to the mailbox to check every day, and he'll continue being disap-pointed, listlessly dropping the uncooperative replies onto a pile for Aunt Meryl and me to deal with later.

My grandfather waves off Amanda's thank you. "Call me when it's ready," he says.

"I'm sorry," I whisper to her when he's gone.

"Don't be ridiculous," she says. "He's adorable."

"Tell that to my brothers," I grumble. "Maybe if they'd seen it that way, they'd have stuck around."

Amanda's eyes linger on me, but she doesn't say anything else.

"So," Amanda says, as she starts cutting up pineapple. "Now that we're here, you might as well tell us *everything*. I mean, everything we can't see from watching the video!" She emits a sound that definitely qualifies as a squeal.

"You know there's no squealing," I remind her. "I can kick you out. And keep the food."

Amanda snorts. In her own way, she's defiantly who she is, which is what I love best about her, even if sometimes she and I don't exactly see the world the same way.

"You're famous!" Lucy says. "You look so amazing in that video. You're all glowy!"

"Pretty sure the glowy was just your makeup job and the lighting in the restaurant."

"And his viewers are soooo shipping you two," Imani says.

"The shipping is pretty dang cute," Jessa agrees. "So much for 'don't read the comments.'"

That's one thing I feel super lucky about. Maybe it's because Bear's not an A-list celebrity, but we don't seem to have gotten the usual barrage of hate-comments about what the hell he sees in me or that he could do better. Most people think we're cute, the perfect couple—*so outdoorsy! And they both love food!* Not that there aren't haters—there are a few—but I feel like I can ignore them.

What I can't ignore is how weird it makes me feel to be shipped with Bear by thousands of people when I don't know if it's actually what I *want*.

That kiss. It was so...

It was so *not* the other kiss.

"So...?" Rachel asks. "Was it all that and a bag of chips?"

All their eyes are on me, their faces lit and expectant, and...

I don't lie. Like, ever.

Mostly because I'm the world's worst liar. I think I was born without the gene that lets you arrange your face for public consumption. Mine tells everyone the truth instantly.

But I have to try, because if I don't, there will be a million questions.

What do you mean it was *okay*?

I mean, you like him, right?

Hanna? You like *him*, right?

And knowing them, they will somehow manage to pry everything out of me. Not just how shallow things with Bear felt, but also...

Kissing practice.

Which didn't feel like practice at all. It felt like The Real Thing in a way not much else has in my life.

That's the *last* thing I want to have to explain to the eager-eyed women crowded around me.

"It was fun!" I say, as buoyantly as possible.

There's a collective sigh of relief, and I realize: They wanted this date to go well almost more than I did. It's a strangely heart-warming realization, how much my friends care about me, even if they don't always... *get* me.

I give them a skeletal outline of the evening, focusing on the food, on how much I enjoyed the restaurant, on the kiss itself, and not all the staging that preceded it or the editing that came afterwards, or the comparative study my mind can't stop making.

Apparently, my acting skills are better than I would have guessed, because no one questions my narrative. And when Amanda pulls out the video for us to watch again—my third time watching—my enthusiasm for the kiss looks pretty great on camera.

So maybe I *can* lie when I'm sufficiently motivated.

I'll admit, the first thing I thought when I saw the finished video, was that Easton would see it too. He'd see the eager look on my face and the way I closed my eyes at the last minute, leaning into Bear and coasting my hand into his soft hair.

Take that, Mr. *I Can't Do This*. This guy *can*.

Not that Easton cares, one way or the other. But still.

22

EASTON

"Hanna's in the kitchen," Brody tells me, greeting me at Gabe's front door as I mount the porch steps. Pretty much all the Wilder gatherings take place at Gabe's, although now that Brody and Rachel have their new place, we do occasionally gather there.

"I didn't ask," I grouse.

He smiles. "I just thought you might want to know."

"You might want to set your expectations lower. This isn't going to be some big ol' happily ever after. Have you *seen* the video?"

"I saw it," Brody says, with a shrug. "I've seen people kiss their dogs with more passion than she put into that kiss."

I want him to be right. I want it so bad.

Brody's eyes are tight on my face. "How many times did you watch it, East?"

I shake my head.

"Three?"

I jerk my thumb upwards.

"Are you a total glutton for punishment?"

"I just—"

I couldn't make myself stop. I was searching for something, some kind of sign, some kind of proof that this wasn't what was supposed to be happening. I felt like maybe if I watched it enough times, she'd jerk away. Or her eyes would meet mine in some kind of secret glance.

"Do you still think I should talk to her? Even now that the entire world is shipping them?"

Brody's gaze drops away from mine.

"You don't, do you? You think I should let her have this. Damn it."

"I didn't say that. You have to trust your gut. Do what you can live with. You know her better than anyone."

"I know it looked like she was into that kiss, no matter what you think you see."

"I don't know, dude. I'm… I'm sorry."

There's not much else to say, so the two of us turn and go inside. Brody heads into the living room and I turn toward the kitchen, but before I reach it, I hear Lucy say, "I mean if he wanted the whole world to see that video, I guess he's definitely interested."

"Guess so," Hanna says back, her voice oddly, unusually, buoyant.

I step in. No matter how weird things might be between us, I've got an envelope full of flyers we need to split up and distribute.

"Oh, hey, Easton," Lucy says, as Amanda gives me a sideways hug of greeting. Buck, Lucy and Gabe's dog, is tucked under Lucy's fingers, accepting scritches as if they're his due.

Hanna looks up. Her eyes are cool, disinterested.

"I have—flyers," I say.

It's not my most brilliant line.

She takes the envelope from me, opens it, examines the flyers, and nods. "They look fine."

"I thought I could distribute half, and you could distribute the other half."

"That works."

Hanna sets the envelope on a chair. I can feel her not looking at me as hard as I'm not looking at her. "Aren't you going to ask me how my date went?"

Amanda's eyes flick from her face to mine.

"I saw the video," I say. "Looks like it went well."

"It did. Really well." She picks up a plate full of food. "I'm going out on the deck. Anyone else?"

"I'll go," Lucy says.

That leaves Amanda and me in the kitchen. Amanda looks at Hanna's retreating back. Then at me. She gives me a quizzical little raise of her eyebrow. "You okay?" she asks quietly.

"Fine."

"You want to talk about it?"

I shake my head.

"So then, you'll just let me speculate?"

"You're the worst," I tell her. "Can't a guy just have an off day?"

"Not an off day when you don't give Hanna a hard time about her date with a guy named *Bear*. Where is he, by the way? Didn't anyone invite him?"

"I assumed Hanna would," I say, which is true, but not

the whole truth. I thought about inviting him to join us, and then, somewhat conveniently, forgot.

"I assumed one of you would," Amanda said, tilting her head.

A cry of rage comes from the deck. "Buck!"

We hurry out to see what's going on, just as Gabe vaults himself off the deck and chases his dog across the yard, yanking something out of Buck's jaw. Whatever it is has not fared well.

Gabe holds it aloft, triumphant, and I recognize it. It's one of the flyers advertising Bear's next workshop. Buck must have snatched it off the kitchen chair where Hanna set it.

"Whose is this?" Gabe demands.

"I brought a stack of them to give to Hanna," I say. "We're a few short on registrations for the later sessions and I wanted to get them up around town sometime in the next few days."

"Don't," Lucy tells Gabe. She turns to us. "He has this obsession."

"Oh, I know all about his obsession," I say. "Buck chewed Lucy's sweatshirt, and Rachel's dildo—"

This is not as outrageous a thing to say in mixed company as it sounds. Rachel is a sex therapist, and she runs sex toy parties on a regular basis with a focus on helping people with their sexual issues. Buck got hold of a bright purple glitter dildo of hers, and the rest was not so much history as purple glitter barf.

"—and my sweater," Jessa says.

"—and my shoe," Mari says.

"Wait, so, what's the upshot?" Geneva, my mom's girlfriend, asks.

"The upshot is that when Buck chews something belonging to a Wilder family member's significant other, that significant other is here to stay. Buck is a prognosticator of Wilder romantic success."

Geneva squints. "So, like, when Buck had to have surgery because of my sock?"

"I didn't know about that," my mom says, reaching for Geneva's hand.

Lucy closes her eyes. Tight.

"It's a miracle Buck has survived this long," Amanda says grimly.

"I mean, so are the flyers yours? East? Because you brought them here. Right? But that doesn't make any sense." Gabe is talking to himself. "They would have to be a woman's. Hanna's, because you were going to give them to her?"

"Gabe," Lucy warns, but Gabe is deep into his theory now. You can practically see his thoughts whizzing.

"Or Bear's!" Gabe says, his face lighting up, his eyes going to Hanna, curious.

She won't look at him.

Brody's eyes find mine. Amanda's, too. Because the flyers, of course, are Bear's. They were made to advertise Bear's workshop.

Not that I put any stock in Gabe's wild hair about Buck predicting true love.

Still, my stomach feels sour and wrong. Because the flyers are clearly Bear's, and the implication is, clearly, that Buck has picked Bear for Hanna.

"The whole thing is bullshit."

We all turn to look at Hanna.

Her arms are crossed, her brows lowered, a deep scowl written into her face.

"You really think a dog can predict who's going to fall in love with anyone? No way. The flyers don't *belong* to anyone. The whole thing is stupid."

She gets up, sets her plate on the bench, and storms off the deck and around the house. I'm on my feet, but before I even reach the steps, a truck engine growls from out front, and then tires skid on gravel as she peels out.

"Easton, maybe not right now—" Brody says, but he's talking to my back as I round the corner and head for my Jeep.

23

───────

HANNA

I've just stepped down from the truck and started toward my house when I hear the crunch of tires behind me, on the driveway. I turn, wondering why my granddad's back, hours early from his fishing trip. But it's not my granddad. It's Easton's Jeep, moving a little too fast; he screeches to a stop next to my truck, cuts the engine, and jumps out.

I turn away and start toward the door.

He grabs my arm. "Hanna, wait."

I shake myself free. "Don't."

"Han, I'm sorry."

I scowl at the ground. "That just makes it worse. You are *not* allowed to be sorry. I'm the one who broke our friendship with dumb kissing practice. I have no idea what I was thinking. Although—" I turn on him, rage winning out over hurt again, "—you shouldn't have said yes if you couldn't handle it!"

"I know." His voice is quiet, low and rough.

"But of course, you don't want to be kissing me, and I should never have pressured you."

"Hanna—"

"Tell me it's not permanently broken though. You didn't even ask how my date went. And then you didn't make fun of me at all. I can't deal with you if you're going to be super weird about this."

"Hanna, I—"

"You know what? No. Just, no. I don't want to hear it. Can't we just pretend it never happened? Can't we just rewind back to before it happened?"

"I don't know if I can—"

"Shut *up*. Just shut up. Don't say you can't. Just—be my friend, okay?"

My heart pounds, louder than the rush of the river in its bed. If he says he can't—

I don't know. I can't even think it.

"I can… do that."

I finally let myself look up at him, and I feel an overwhelming sense of relief, because he's smiling. Not a full-blown smile, but the one that sneaks through when he's trying not to.

But then the smile slips off his face, and he's just… looking at me. And it scares me, that look, because I don't know what it means, and everything feels so brittle.

"What?" I demand.

Easton rakes a hand through his hair. "Han. You're my best friend. I'd never want to do anything to endanger that."

Warmth floods my chest. Because I'm not that girl, if you know what I mean. I never had a *best* friend growing up, the one who picked me first and played with me at recess. I had brothers, instead, and I wanted to be one of them, and I mostly was, although there was always a small part of me that knew I would never, quite. Just like I'll never, quite, be a Wilder, like I'll never, quite, be a member of the sisterhood of Wilder women. And it's always been mostly OK. I've always been mostly OK.

I didn't know until this second how much I wanted this.

Easton chuckles. "That's fine. Don't say it back. Leave me hanging. I get it. You can do better."

"No," I say, recovering. "You're..."

"Can't do it, can you?"

"It does cause me physical pain." There's a tease in my voice, but I don't feel like joking, not right now. I swallow. Hard. "You're my best friend, too."

It sounds rough and uneven, like someone navigating unfamiliar terrain... which I guess I'm trying to do.

We're both quiet for a long time. I fidget with the ring of keys in my hand, but there's also an unfamiliar bubble of pleasure in my chest. His best friend. I'm his best friend.

And it's still not enough.

Under the happiness is another emotion, thorny and twisted.

Greed.

I want more.

Stop it, Han. This is enough. It has to be.

Easton toes the earth with his fancy-looking sneaker. "Is it too late to ask how your date went?"

"Yup. That ship sailed." I cross my arms.

He snorts. "You know you want to tell me." His voice holds the old, familiar mockery.

It's a relief to hear it.

"Why, so you can give me a hard time?"

"Why would I do that?" he asks innocently. "Is there something *damning* in your story?"

Yes.

"No."

"Then what will I give you a hard time about?"

I cock my head. This is our old game, but I don't feel like the same old Hanna, not quite. "When do you not give me a hard time?"

"What if I promise not to?"

I squint at him.

"Pinky swear."

I put on an old West drawl. "Your pinky swear's no good here."

I sneak a peek his way. He's definitely smiling now. So am I.

He tilts his head. "What if we take it one element at a time. Super fancy restaurant?"

This is Easton, getting his way somehow. Making an end run around my defenses.

"The food was fantastic," I admit.

"Dressing up and wearing makeup?"

I squelch a smile. "I didn't hate it as much as you'd think."

"Being on camera?"

"Cypress's really good at their job. They made me feel really comfortable."

Like you do, I think. *Or like you used to, before I discovered how much I want to smush my face into yours.*

If he can hear the loud voice in my head, he doesn't

show it. "Let's try some harder questions," he says. "How was the company? Cypress aside. What's Bear like?"

"He's a nice guy. Interesting. Lots of stuff to say. Never at a loss for stories to tell."

His eyebrows draw together. "Is that *good?* Or *bad*?"

"It's good, I guess?"

"You guess? Did you have fun?"

"Yeah?"

"Hanna," he says. "I think I'm missing something here."

Yeah. I think he's missing something here, too. And suddenly I'm so tired. Tired of holding back, tired of protecting myself, tired of resisting what I want.

"You haven't asked the really hard questions yet," I inform him.

"What are those?"

"The *after* questions."

He gets quiet. It's not just that he doesn't say anything. His whole body gets quiet. Still. Like he's afraid if he moves or speaks, he'll break something.

Maybe he will.

Or maybe I will.

Maybe we will.

"Okay," he says slowly. "Afterwards. Did it happen like we guessed? Did he go in for a kiss outside the car?"

I nod. "Yeah. He waited a minute, though, so Cypress could set up."

"He *staged* it?" Easton's outrage is purifying.

I feel instantly better. "Yeah."

"No," he says. "He. Did. Not."

"He did," I say, but it doesn't actually sting to think about it this time. That's the power of Easton. He makes things not so heavy. Like he's just lifted it off my shoulders and I can…

"Are you laughing?" he says. "Because there is *nothing* funny about that. What a… camera whore! Jesus. I hope, at least, that it was *worth* it?"

Here it comes; here we go.

"No," I say.

His face wrinkles in confusion; that wasn't the answer he was expecting. "Not worth it?"

I shake my head.

"Not a good kiss?" There are fine wrinkle lines between his brows.

"It was *fine*," I say.

I can see the moment when he understands. When the wrinkles disappear, and the corner of his mouth turns up.

It's that almost invisible quirk of a smile that gives me the first glimmer of hope.

"But?" he asks, drawing the word out.

I force myself to meet his eyes. He's watching me. Intently.

His eyes are so dark I can only see a rim of green, and they hold mine, a fierce need shining in them.

Heat streaks through me, lighting up corners and edges. It gives me courage.

Maybe we'll break, or maybe we'll bend. I can't know if I don't try.

"I think you spoiled me," I whisper.

24

EASTON

She pulls her gaze from mine, and I know I have a split second before she turns away or laughs it off, and I don't hesitate, I reach for her. I wrap her wrists in my hands—they're surprisingly small in my grasp —and tug her towards me. She trips over her feet and makes a quiet, startled sound, her eyes finding mine again, lit up and curious, but not scared. Eager. And then her gaze drops to my mouth, and I watch her pupils flare, and blood rushes through my veins, demanding.

I capture the curve of her head in my hands and lower my mouth to hers.

Even though it's the second time, it feels like the first. Because everything's on the line. Because I'm putting myself—and our friendship—on a cliff's edge.

And it feels like falling, without a net, without the hope of a parachute, until she groans against my lips and opens to my probing tongue.

I growl and delve deeper, needing more, needing so much it's an all-over ache.

She crowds close to me, pressing her body against mine, and I let myself relish it completely this time, soaking up the feel of her. Soft and round and full. My hands drop from behind her head and explore her, curves and hills and valleys, all perfectly her, filling my hands and my mind, crowding out sanity and good sense. And she likes it; she presses back against my touch, stirs and stretches like a cat into my palm, everywhere it travels.

I can't help myself; I glide my touch up to cup a breast, her nipple tight as I brush over it. I reach for the hem of her shirt, torn between having more of her lips and sealing my mouth over that nipple so I can tease her with flicks of my tongue.

Except as I'm reaching for the hem of her shirt, she steps back, breaking the kiss. She turns away.

"Hanna."

"I just—why now? Just because someone else wants me?"

The question—the question I've asked myself and my brother and the powers that be—catches me off guard, and I hesitate a moment too long. Her body language collapses. "If this is a competition or a joke or something to you—"

We're in totally uncharted territory. I could disappoint her so easily. I'm not a celebrity chef survivalist forager, big enough to toss her over my shoulder and ballsy enough to do it on television. I've never been anyone's anything, in truth, except for brother and son. Every role I've ever played has been locked in from birth, given to me on a silver platter, and even the people who love me most don't take me seriously. And there might be a reason for that. All I know how to do is joke around.

I take a deep breath.

"It's not a competition, and it's not a joke."

She freezes, slowly turning back toward me.

"And yes, it did start when you started trying to win over Bear, but only because that was the first time I let myself—" I close my eyes. "See you," I finish. "Or maybe," I amend, thinking of our shopping trip, "maybe it was the first time you saw yourself."

"What are you talking about?"

"I'm talking about you. Standing in front of that mirror in that dressing room and looking so goddamn edible that—"

She tilts her head, and for the first time, looks amused. "That? That what?"

I scowl.

"Easton."

"I may or may not have fantasized about you later. I..." Too much? I discover I don't care. "Jerked off, thinking about how good you looked."

"Easton!" she says, mock outraged. But obviously pleased. She ducks her head. "Me too," she whispers. "I mean, not how good I looked. But you know. The way you looked at me."

My mouth falls open.

"What?!" she demands. "You think I *don't*?"

I grin, because she's so very, very Hanna. Ready to go to the mat even when we're cracking open our sexual selves for each other. "I didn't say that. I just wasn't expecting you to, I don't know, say it." I'm temporarily floored—except for my cock, which is the opposite of floored—by this new piece of information. And all the accompanying images. And how much I want to see that happening in practice.

"Easton?" she asks.

"Sorry. Distracted with the *picturing*," I tell her. "Feel free to share any more relevant info along those lines."

The corners of her mouth tip up.

But I still haven't addressed her fear. Not *really*.

"I can't promise nothing bad will happen," I tell her. "But I've been feeling this way for a while, and it's not a game or a joke or a competition to me. If Bear walked away tomorrow, I'd still want to kiss you more than I want to draw my next breath."

"Oh," Hanna says. "Oh."

Her cheeks get pinker, and my cock gets harder. "Is that a 'me too?'"

"I mean… yes? But also…" She scuffs her Converse sneaker into the driveway. "This feels like, objectively, a terrible idea."

That's a bucket of ice water over my head, because—as I told Brody—I know she's right.

"It's not just our friendship. It's our working relationship. And the way your family sees me. Sex changes things. One of us might catch feelings, and then… then it gets messy. Complicated."

They're almost exactly my words. "Yes," I say carefully. "All those things are true. But also…"

Her eyes are locked on mine. I can see all the indecision, the uncertainty, but also the hope. The excitement.

"I'm not going to stop thinking about it. The way you kiss. The way you *feel*. And I think you want exactly what I want. I know it's been a long time for you, and I know it would be so, so good, the two of us together."

Her pupils are dark. Blown. Her gaze never strays from mine.

"Come here." I open my arms.

She gives me a last, suspicious glance, and it makes me laugh, because it's so Hanna, and I like her so goddamn much. And then she steps forward and lets me hold her, hug her, and I wrap her up and try to reassure her with the strength of my embrace and the truth my body wants to tell hers.

"I could make you feel so good," I murmur against her hair, loving the brush of those short, silky strands against my lips. I want to explore every texture of her. Now. "And I really, really want to."

25

HANNA

My whole body says yes. And I'm only exaggerating a little. Technically, my toes are not really involved, or my teeth. But all sorts of bits and pieces of me that you might not expect are. Easton's body has the key to mine, and when he's this close—holding me, whispering teasing words in my ear—I'm on.

Even though I think I'm probably right, that this will end badly, that I will lose all kinds of things that matter to me, I want that *yes* in a way I have never wanted anything before.

I tilt my chin up so our mouths slide together like key and lock. And oh my God, it's so good. Easton kisses like it's his professional obligation and the only thing on his mind. He kisses with his lips and his tongue and the rough noise of pleasure in his chest and his hands all over my body like he can't get enough.

"You—" he says, when we tug apart momentarily, both panting. "—are the hottest woman I have ever kissed."

I roll my eyes.

"Don't roll your eyes at me."

"That's gotta be panty-melter bullshit," I tell him.

"It's not," he says fervently, gently planting a line of kisses along my jaw, sending tendrils of pleasure everywhere.

I consider fighting him more, but the kisses skate down my throat, into the deep scoop of my top.

"Please don't ever stop wearing these scoop-necked tops," he growls as his tongue teases the neckline, and I decide that if I'll be rewarded like this, I can give him what he wants.

His fingertips follow his tongue, nudging the neckline even lower, his mouth on the top curve of my breast making me limp with need. "I love your body. I feel like your body is made for me." His voice is so rough I can feel it on all my nerve endings.

My hands roam his body, too, over lean, hard muscle, broad shoulders, thick biceps, sinewy forearms. I need to touch him everywhere I possibly can in case this is the only time. I need to store him up. I'm greedy, and he's beautiful, even more beautiful to touch than to look at. I can't get enough.

"May I?" he says, tugging at the hem of my shirt.

It's testament to how far gone I am that I don't hesitate before pulling it over my head, even though we're outside.

The look on Easton's face when he sees me shirtless makes it completely worth it. He looks at me the way most people look at the Grand Canyon or the Sistine Chapel or whatever it is they've waited a lifetime to feast their eyes on.

No one has *ever* looked at me like that. Like he wants to devour me. Like he wants to possess me.

It makes my legs go watery. But not as watery as they get when he closes the gap between us, pushes the cup of my bra down to expose my nipple, and bends his head to tease it. Then my knees actually buckle.

He catches me, clutches me, his mouth never stopping its work. And somehow, he manages to support my weight against him and also work a hand down between my legs, cupping my mound, giving me the palm of his hand to rub against my now slightly damp leggings.

Which is, unfortunately, when sanity shows up for me.

"Easton."

"Mmmph," he says.

"Easton. You have to stop. I need to tell Bear I'm not interested. I mean, not that I promised him anything, or like we talked about exclusivity. But, you know, out of respect. Close that... loop."

He surfaces, eyes glazed and mouth slick. "Oh, shit. Yeah. You do. And..." Apparently sanity has come to him, too. "He's going to *hate* me. I told him we weren't... that I didn't..." His eyes rake over me—face, lingering on my mouth, throat, bare breast, disheveled bra. "Turns out I lied to him." He grins wolfishly, which sets up a slow pulse in my core. "Because there is definitely something going on between us."

I smile. "Well. I gotta tell him the truth. If... we're going to keep kissing."

He reaches out and smooths his thumb over my lower lip; my tongue comes out, involuntarily, to touch it, and he groans. "We're definitely going to keep kissing. And I'm hoping a bunch of other stuff, too."

"Sex?" I blurt.

He grins. "If you want that."

"I do. I really, really do. You have absolutely no idea how bad my drought has been. I don't think I want to tell you how long it's been since I last had sex." At least five years. I don't want to count any more exactly than that.

He eyes me, his lips still glossy from ministering to my nipple. "I really, really, wish you hadn't said that. Because now all I can think about is fixing that." His gaze skates over me, snagging on my mouth, the vee of my leggings, and my nipples—hard and visible through the lace of my bra.

"So, sex, definitely," I tease, and enjoy how his eyes darken more. It's such a high to be on the receiving end of his attention.

He reaches for me, but I pull back. "Probably not the best idea?" I say wryly.

"Probably not," he agrees. "What are you going to tell Bear?"

"I think... for now I'll just tell him I'm not interested in taking things between him and me any further."

"You can tell him the whole truth if you want to. Don't worry about me."

"Nah," I say. "That feels... complicated."

There's a flare of something behind his eyes. "What's complicated?"

"Trying to explain what this *is*. It just feels complicated to try to explain it to someone else." I shiver suddenly, my skin cooling as the sun kisses the mountains in the distance. I reassemble myself, pulling my bra cup up, tugging my t-shirt over my head.

He watches me, his eyes unreadable. "Yeah. I get that.

So maybe... we don't try to define it for now. You just let me break your sex fast... and enjoy it."

Then he slides a hand behind my head and draws me close, the kiss feeling more and more perfectly inevitable until his mouth closes tenderly on mine.

26

EASTON

When I let her go this time—long before I want to, my head still full of all the ways I need to touch her, my cock flushed so full it aches—she says, "We're going to have sex!"

It makes me laugh. She's so delighted with herself, with us. She's fucking adorable, this Hanna. "Oh, yes, we definitely are," I tell her.

She gets up on tiptoes, reaching for another kiss, the first one she's initiated, and I adore that, too. Also the way her mouth opens immediately beneath mine, and the little breath she sighs out, and the way her hand clutches at my clothes before finding where it wants to be, which is apparently my ass. No complaints here, except maybe that I wish we were naked and in my bedroom.

I pull her tight up against me and let her feel exactly what she does to me, while I find her nipple again through her shirt and bra. I already know she likes just the tip teased, the flick of my finger over the hard bead.

"Oh my God, E. It's so *good.*"

What I'm learning is that Hanna's bluntness is especially delightful when it comes to physical pleasure. She's honest, and I love that she tells it like it is, in this arena as in all others. "Yeah," I say. "It's really fucking good."

"And I'm so sex starved," she breathes, smoothing a hand down over the bulge in the front of my shorts.

"Hanna," I groan, going in for another kiss, even though we said we were going to stop until she calls off the thing with Bear, if it's even a thing. But she's so delicious; I want handfuls of her. She makes me So. Fucking. Greedy.

And the garden scent of her, in contrast with all the ways she's so down to earth? Makes me completely insane.

"You're perfect," I tell her.

That makes her laugh. "So, you don't want to change anything about me."

"Nope."

"Even though you once told your brothers that if you ever turned up dead, they should have me arrested and held without bail? And even though you once said that my business card should say Thorn in Easton's Side?"

"Did *I* say that?"

"It was a while ago," she admits.

I take my phone out.

"What are you doing?"

"Putting in a VistaPrint order for your business cards. Is that a capital 's' in 'side'?"

She swats at the phone; I grab her wrist and our eyes meet, heat flaring in hers. I pull her close and kiss her, a smacking joke of a kiss that isn't a joke at all. Even the short, silly contact sends need surging up my spine.

"I like it," I tell her. "All of it."

What I've spent the last hour realizing is that there's a straight connection from the way we poke each other to my libido. And I think there's at least a chance it's true for her too. So, all the teasing? It's been the best kind of foreplay.

"What?"

"I like you the way you are."

"Really," she says, crossing her arms. "You liked the old baggy clothes?"

I grin at her. "I like all your clothes. I like the new ones because I can see more of your body, and I really like seeing more of your body. I would like to see a lot more of your body."

Her eyes darken, and my cock throbs.

"And I meant what I said, that the whole world should see more of you. Everyone should see how good you look. But also?"

I pause for effect.

She tilts her head, waiting.

"I don't want anyone else to know how fucking hot you are, including Bear fucking Warden because I want you to myself."

"Yeah?" she says, blushing. She raises an eyebrow, looking immensely pleased with herself. She obviously knows her sexual power, and for some reason, that makes me insanely happy.

"Yeah."

We watch each other. Careful. Curious. Her mouth slowly curves into a smile that makes a whole fucking garden bloom in my chest.

I wave a hand. "Now I should probably get the hell out

of here before I kiss you again. Because if I do, I can't promise I'm going to stop."

27

HANNA

I don't walk—I float inside.

No, obviously, I don't. I walk. But it feels like I'm floating. I understand now why people talk about *glowing*. I feel like I could power the town of Rush Creek off the energy flowing through my veins. My body shines, bright and alive.

I'm going to have *really good sex*!

This is definitely something to be ecstatic about.

I head to my room and try to harness my scattered energy so I can do some online research. Foraging in Central Oregon is my topic—but it's like trying to educate a classroom full of chipmunks. I fall down a YouTube hole, starting with stinging nettles and non-poisonous mushrooms and seamlessly slipping into using hair to stitch a wound.

Many lost hours and lots of sketchy medical advice later, my granddad comes back from his fishing trip, banging through the front door. A few minutes later, he bellows my name.

I step into the living room and discover him pacing, eyes lit up, throwing off agitated energy. The coffee table is strewn with party invitations—RSVP cards separated from envelopes and tossed everywhere. He's obviously been double checking to make sure my brothers really didn't respond.

There's a look on his face—thoughtful, almost mischievous. He looks like trouble. I saw that look on enough Hott brother faces during my childhood to recognize it.

I'm worried about what's in store for me, but also relieved, because there's no way he'll notice my moony distraction.

"No RSVPs from your brothers," he says.

"No," I agree, the single syllable drawn out and wary.

"I have a plan. I need you to email them."

"You have a… plan?"

He nods. "We're going to do like the Wilders do."

My mouth drops open. "What?"

"They aren't sitting on their asses, twiddling their thumbs, agonizing about how the rodeo days are over and men don't come here anymore to prove they're men."

That's entirely true, although I wouldn't have expected my grandfather to see it so clearly.

"They're changing with the times. They're recognizing that Rush Creek is about weddings and parties and relaxation, not horses and bulls and testosterone."

"True enough," I allow.

If my grandad paces any faster, I'm afraid he's going to hurt himself—or wear a path in the carpet. "Slow down, Granddad."

"We're going to do that, too, just like the Wilders."

"We—"

"You and me and the boys."

"The boys—" I know I sound like a fool, but I can't seem to get my feet fully under me. I've never seen my grandfather this riled up.

"Your brothers. We're going to turn the ranch into a wedding venue and spa."

I gape at him, half horrified, half awed at the extent of his denial. "That will never happen in a million years," I tell him. "The Hott brothers couldn't wait to get out of here. You think they'd come back here to be like the Wilders? To be pinned to this place and a business—"

I stop, mid-sentence, suddenly grasping the full extent of his delusion. "You want *me* to run a wedding venue?"

"You want to have something of your own," he says.

I shake my head. "Not *that*. Frills and lace and veils and flowers and bridezillas and momzillas and ten times more administrivia than adventuring—ugh!"

"If you don't want to do it, you don't have to do it," my granddad says, shrugging. "I'll do it with your brothers."

"They're not coming back!"

My voice is bigger and angrier than I mean it to be, but my granddad doesn't even flinch. "They will if you ask them to. They won't for me, but they will if you ask. They'll show up for the party if you ask them to, and when they do, I'll present my plan, and they'll see. They'll see that they owe it to you to take care of you."

"I don't *need* taking care of." I've gotten my voice under control again, and it emerges tight but steady.

"Maybe not, but they owe it to you to make sure you have something of your own, and they owe it to the land to turn it into something useful. And they owe it to me…"

He gets very quiet.

For the first time, I see how tight his mouth is, how one hand clutches the other to still its shaking.

"Granddad," I say gently.

He looks away. If I didn't know him better, I'd guess he was trying to hide tears—but that's impossible.

"I owe it to them to leave them something."

Oh, this impossible, idiotic, deluded old man, who I can't help loving, because despite everything, he's got a soft caramel core.

"Granddad," I repeat. "If you do that way, they're not going to get it. They're going to see it as an attempt to control them. To get them back to Rush Creek, when all any of them ever wanted was to get out of here and see the big, bad world."

"Well, they've seen it!" he says. "It's time for them to come back and claim their inheritance. Settle down. Be there for you."

"I don't need them to be here for me," I attempt, but there's no getting through to him when he's like this.

"Email them," he repeats.

"I—"

His shoulders slump slightly, and suddenly he looks his age. And even though he can make me bananas, and his grumpy old man act drove my brothers out of Rush Creek, I want what he wants, and I can't say no.

I START several emails to my brothers.

HEY, Tuck,

Granddad wanted me to reach out and...

TUCKER—

Zero pressure but

TUCK,

Miss you! Hope you're thinking about heading this way for granddad's...

TUCK,

You absolute asshole, where have you been?!

I DROP the phone on the bed, collapse back on the pillow. Something pokes my spine, and from underneath me I draw Leonard, the pink teddy bear. "What do you think, dude? Is Granddad nuts? They're not coming, right? No fucking way."

Leonard stares back at me, black button eyes unwavering.

"You're not helping, bud," I tell him.

I pick up my phone again. Drop it. Pick it up.

I text, *My granddad wants me to email my brothers and*

invite them to his eighty-fifth. Before I can think better of it, I hit send.

Easton and I don't text. But then again, Easton and I don't kiss. It's a week for unprecedented experiences, so why not throw one more in there?

Three dots appear, and my heart goes wild. I clutch the phone, waiting for his answer, thinking, *Who are you and what have you done with Hanna?*

You don't know how many times I typed and erased 'new phone, who dis?' Easton texts back, which makes me laugh, easing the tightness in my chest. *Do you *want* to email them?*

I don't know. Sort of? My granddad wants to turn the ranch into a wedding venue and spa.

Three dots appear.

Vanish.

Appear.

Vanish.

"My sentiments *exactly*," I tell Leonard and my phone.

Easton's text pops up: *It's not the worst idea ever.*

No. It isn't. Which I think is part of what's causing the tightness in my chest and the confusion in my head.

I think it's a pretty good idea, I text him back. *But he wants me to get my brothers here to do it. He wants me to email them and make them come for the party so he can present his idea... and then somehow, they're supposed to bow to family duty or their love of the land, or something, and give up their big dreams.*

They might say no.

But they might say yes.

It's ambitious, it would be a huge amount of work... and it might just be a success.

I tap out another text. *What do you think? Should I do it?*

28

EASTON

I stretch out on the couch with my phone in my hand, feeling so much it's hard to sit still. I'm not the kind of guy who you'd catch dancing around his apartment in celebration or anything, but I now feel like a few fist pumps and a beer might be in order.

Hanna.

Hanna is...

Amazing.

I mean I knew that. I knew it from looking at her, from spending more time around her these last few weeks.

But I didn't *know it* know it, the way I know it now. Not until I had her in my arms, fierce and eager...

And I didn't know how good it would feel to know there was going to be more of that.

We're going to have sex! (As Hanna would say.)

I mean, who would have thought that a guy who has pretty much always had as much sex as he wanted, with more or less whomever he wanted, would be so excited?

I am, though.

And now she's *texting* me, *asking my opinion about something that matters*, and, not gonna lie, it feels like I've bet on the winning 100:1 underdog in Vegas and dug up pirate treasure in my backyard and…

Apparently, I lied about the not dancing around my living room, because I press play on Imagine Dragons' "On Top of the World" and do a victory dance for a minute before plopping back down on the couch.

I reread the last bit of our text exchange about her brothers.

Don't do anything that makes you uncomfortable, I'd texted her.

It's complicated, she'd texted back.

I know Hanna doesn't love things that are complicated, any more than I do, and I know no one loves trying to text about things that are complicated, so I hit the call button.

"Complicated how?"

"Do you really want to know?" Hanna's voice is low, quiet, and slightly throaty.

"Yeah. If you want to tell me." *What I really mean is, Keep talking. Please. Tell me.* Because it turns out that I don't just want more of Hanna's body. I want more of all of Hanna. It's a hunger, heat, all through me.

That thought sets off a small pulse of alarm, but I push it aside.

"I don't know where to start."

"At the beginning?"

She takes a deep breath. "My brothers and I were close. As kids. Free range, you know? Always outside, working some, yeah, but running in the woods, too. I was one of the boys. My mom wanted me to be her little girl, but I didn't want to. I wanted to be a Hott *brother*."

That was probably what had made Hanna so tough, what had made her the kind of girl who kicked my friends' and my asses at keep-away and then trash-talked us afterwards.

"My dad was different, though," she says, and fondness creeps into her voice. "You know my brothers and I had different dads, right?"

"Yeah. Yours was that big-time barrel racer."

"Who left," she says flatly.

I'd known that, just from the way you absorb stuff that happens in a small town. Everyone kinda knew... but for a town where everything was fodder for gossip, no one talked much about it.

"My dad—he was different from my mom. He didn't give a shit if I was girl, boy, or horse. He just made it clear he loved the shit out of me. When he was around, which wasn't that often. He talked about settling down, but the road always called him back in the end. And then he left for good when I was seven. We didn't hear from him after that. When I was in high school, I found out he was killed on the circuit."

A knot forms in my chest. "Shit," I say. "I didn't know that part."

"Yeah. Well. By then it wasn't like I thought he was coming back."

I can hear everything in her voice. How hard she's trying to sound like she doesn't care, and the hairline fractures in her voice that tell me she does.

"He was the first one to leave and not come back, but he

wasn't the last. Then my mom… went. And I think my brothers just got sick of it, of men who didn't stick around, of losing people they cared about, Rush Creek fussing over them. Whatever it was, they left, too, one after the other. Seeking their fortunes, following their dreams, whatever."

I want to tell her she doesn't have to be stoic with me, but I know Hanna too well for that, so all I say—again—is, "That sucks."

"Yeah," she agrees.

We're both quiet for a moment.

"So, your brothers all went off to seek their fortunes."

"Mmm-hmm. They had bigger dreams than Rush Creek, and they all got what they wanted. Movie star, financial genius, brilliant scientist, big-time lawyer, bodyguard—and now they're too busy for me and Granddad and the ranch."

I can hear hurt in her voice, and more than anything, I want to wrap her up and hold her tight and do anything—everything—to soothe her.

"Hey. If my opinion means anything—"

"You know it doesn't," she says, laughing.

Except—I think, with a twinge of pleasure—I know it *does*, because she asked, and she doesn't ask other people's opinions. "I'd say go ahead and email them. What do you have to lose?"

"You mean besides my pride?"

"Overrated," I say. "I just swallowed mine earlier today and admitted how much I want this girl…"

"You didn't have much pride to begin with," she teases.

Yeah, teasing is definitely foreplay, or so my cock says.

"Hey," I say. "If you, um, need a date to that eighty-fifth birthday party?"

"Yeah?" she says, and I can hear a smile in her voice, which makes me ridiculously, absurdly, happy.

"I'm your man."

When she says, shyly, "I'd like that," I have to do a second, silent victory dance to celebrate.

HANNA

"Hey," I say, letting the door of Wilder HQ swing shut.

It's Thursday night, and I'm not supposed to be in the office, but I knew I'd find Bear here. He'd mentioned that he wanted to pull some additional cooking supplies from our stash for the next trip, scheduled to start Friday afternoon.

He looks up from where he's bent over a tub of light-weight pots and pans. "Oh, hey, Hanna!" He beams at me. "My viewers *loved* the date video, did you see?" He straightens and pulls his phone out of his back pocket. "Now we'll definitely have to go out again. We can't disappoint them, right?" His eyes dance, and his tone is teasing, but...

He means it—I can tell. He wants to go out again, or as much as Bear Warden wants anything aside from the limelight.

I bite my lip. "About that..."

The smile slides off Bear's face. I have zero chill, and my

face—and voice—broadcast my emotions, no matter how hard I try to keep them from doing so. It's especially aggravating because I find it hard to read other people's expressions. They're often closed books to me... and I'm wide open.

"You're an awesome guy," I begin. "You're good-looking and smart and ambitious—"

He slumps. "You don't have to do that. Butter me up. I know the speech. And it ends with, 'It's not you, it's me,' right?"

He doesn't sound angry or unkind, just... disappointed.

"Uh, yeah," I admit.

I'm about to say that it's not really him *or* me, it's *us,* or the lack of us, but he tilts his head to one side. "Dang," he says. "I had a good time."

"I'm—"

"Don't say you're sorry," he says, holding up a hand. "That's the *worst.*" His forehead wrinkles. "Oh, man! My viewers are going to be *bummed.*" His eyes meet mine. "Honestly, I'm pretty bummed."

I feel bad, but... "You told me not to say I'm sorry," I point out.

That makes him laugh, a little sadly. "I did, didn't I?" He sighs.

"I hope it's not going to be too weird, with us, you know, working together? I can ask Gabe if someone else could—"

He waves it off. "I'm a big boy," he says. "Don't worry about me. Assuming you're OK with continuing to work with me."

"Yeah. Not a problem."

We stand there awkwardly for a moment. I indicate the

storage tote in front of me. "Do you want my help with this?"

"Sure," he says. "Just pull out anything from these tubs that you think might help. We were short on pans, but the real thing I think we needed more of was cooking utensils. Big spoons, spatulas, scrapers—anything you see."

We work for a while in silence. After a while, he says, "Hey, can I ask you something?"

"Sure," I say.

"You and Easton are close, right?"

"Uh, yeah?"

Nerves sizzle in my stomach, because I can't figure out where he's going with this, and I really don't want to be the one to break it to Bear that Easton and I are together.

"Do you think Easton will actually leave his brothers' business and come to Colorado if I offer him this job?" he asks.

I have to run through his words an extra time to make sure they mean what I think they mean. My stomach knots. "I thought... Easton asked you if you'd be willing to consider someone working remotely, and you said you were."

"Oh, yeah. I was, at first. But the more I thought about it, the less I liked that idea, so I made the position on-site. Didn't Easton tell you?"

I shake my head, the stomach-knots turning to rocks.

"I told him I was doing it and asked him if he still wanted to be considered. He said definitely."

I try to breathe around the heavy weight in my belly and the tightness in my chest.

Easton never said anything to me about going to Colorado.

And there's no good reason he should have. Easton doesn't owe me anything. I know who he is, and he knows I know. Whatever's going on between Easton and me, as good as it feels, will be short-lived and neatly tied up with a bow afterwards. That's the Easton Wilder way—and he and I both understand that.

Bear scans my face, and I wonder if I've given myself away. But if he thinks something's weird, he doesn't say it. He shrugs and says, "I was just wondering. Most guys don't want to leave a family business."

"I think Easton has his reasons to want a fresh start," I say, the words short so they don't invite more questions.

"Fair enough," Bear says.

I bend down and dig in the tote in front of me as if it holds the secret to the universe, and for the rest of the time we're working side by side, we talk about camping and food and other topics that don't make my stomach hurt.

30

EASTON

You know in the movies when one character suggests to another that they should hook up? "To get it out of our systems..."?

Well, that's the most ridiculous idea ever in the history of the world.

Because if you're that attracted to someone, chances are that messing around with them is only going to make you more attracted.

Case in point:

It used to be possible for me to be on the same trip as Hanna and not be focused, one hundred percent of the time, on where she was.

Not on this trip.

On this trip, I always know where Hanna is—whether she's helping someone with a pack or offering her GORP to a hiker who didn't pack good snacks or checking maps and compass directions so Bear can focus on being famous and available.

I know how many times she's taken a bio break since we

left the parking area, how much water she has left in her bottles, and how many snack bars she's eaten.

I know that she's wearing a pair of hiking shorts that were doubtless *not* designed to make me crazy, but that bare enough tender thigh to leave me obsessed with the question of what her skin tastes like.

I know that the backpack's chest compression strap is not supposed to make tits look *more* appealing, but Hanna is apparently the exception.

I'm also pretty sure she's avoiding me.

She's not outright ignoring me. She's being friendly. She's just making sure we don't take breaks together or hike near each other.

So when we make camp, I wait for her to choose a tenting site and start setting up. Then I choose the one next to hers.

"Really?" she whispers. "You think that's a good idea?"

"I think it's the best idea I've had all day." I cross my arms and eye her. There's a question I've been wanting—needing—to ask her ever since we got off the phone the other night. "Hanna," I say. "Did you tell Bear that it's over?"

She doesn't look at me. "Yeah," she says. "Yesterday afternoon."

"Why didn't you text me?"

For obvious reasons, I'd wanted to know when Hanna was unencumbered. I'd had this idea that I'd show up at her place with a gift I'd picked out for her. But then she hadn't texted, and I hadn't wanted to seem like I was harassing her to get on with the breakup.

Her fierce gaze tackles mine. "Why didn't you tell me the Bear job meant you would be moving to Colorado?"

I wince. "Oh. He told you that?"

"It was after I told him I didn't want to keep seeing him. We were trying to make not-totally-awkward conversation, and then he asked me if I thought you were really interested in leaving your family's fold, even if it meant going to Colorado."

I won't claim I'd forgotten about the Bear job, but I *had* put it out of my head, probably because my head was filled to the brim with Hanna and what I wanted to do to her. "I'm sorry," I say, meaning it. "Honestly, I haven't been thinking about the job much. I've had other things on my mind."

She casts me a quick mischievous look that makes my blood heat.

"Yes. That," I say. I take a step toward her, but her frown stops me.

"So, you'll take it? If he offers it?"

"I mean... I think so?" I say. All of a sudden it feels like a far more complicated question than it used to.

"So," she briskly responds. "That puts a good end date on this whole thing. Which is handy."

Somehow, I hadn't quite put all the pieces together— the Bear job, relocating to Colorado, things with Hanna. And I don't want to think about all those pieces, not yet— I'm not ready to even admit they all have to be reconciled.

I tug her hand, bringing her closer to me. "Han," I murmur. "I'm not thinking about this *ending*. I'm thinking about it starting. About what I want to do to you tonight when you crawl into my tent. Or when I crawl into yours, if you'd rather."

Her eyes darken and heat. She likes the idea as much as I do.

"Did you pack condoms?" she whispers.

"Mmm-hmm," I hum.

I watch a flush of red peek over the top of her crew-neck, and I want to set my lips right where the red meets the pulse beating in the notch of her collarbone. To lick and suck until she groans.

"But don't rush me," I tell her. "I have lots and lots of things I want to do to you before we'll need condoms."

THE EVENING CRAWLS towards dark and the moment I'll get to kiss Hanna again.

When excusing ourselves for bed finally seems reasonable, she goes first, yawning widely and claiming she was up early, unable to sleep. I wait a respectable fifteen minutes, then make my way to our tents.

"Han," I whisper.

The zipper parts, and I ease inside.

"Hey," she says.

She's sitting cross-legged on her sleeping bag. She changed out of the t-shirt she was wearing earlier and into a clingy light-green tank-top, and as I lower myself to the tent floor, I can't look away from her luscious curves.

"Look at you, beautiful."

She scowls. "Don't."

"Don't what?"

"Don't use the panty-melting skills on me. They don't work on me."

I raise my eyebrows. "At all?"

"At all." Her scowl deepens. "Stop smirking!"

"I'm not smirking."

"You're totally smirking."

I shrug. "Because I like a challenge."

"That's what you got out of what I said? You think that was a *challenge*?"

"Mmm-hmm. Maybe even a bet. I bet you my so-called panty-melting skills work on you, and you bet me they don't. Loser has to get up to make the camp coffee and oatmeal tomorrow morning."

She narrows her eyes. "What's the metric? How do we know if you've won or lost?"

"Oh, you'll know when you've lost."

She looks away, but I see it. The pupil flare and the rising tide of red in her cheeks. And even if she could hide that reaction, her nipples are tight, hard beads under her revealing tank.

"C'mere," I say.

She doesn't move. I scoot myself in and bring my lips so near hers that I can feel her breath on my skin. Then I move away again, gauging her response. Her breathing is quicker now, her mouth falling open a smidge, showing me the inner curve of her lower lip. I bend and test it between my teeth, just a nip to feel if it's as lush and giving as it looks. It is, but even better, I can feel the tension in her body, how hard she's working not to react to me, and it already feels like victory. "Your lip," I tell her. "So fucking soft. I want to lick into your whole mouth. I want to feel every texture. I want you to let me fuck your mouth with my tongue, and I want you to fuck me back."

I settle my mouth against hers, but I don't do what I've just described. I let the kiss be butterfly light, a tease. A torment—I hope.

And gratifyingly, she makes a small, helpless sound.

"You want more?" I tease.

She won't give me the satisfaction of saying yes, but when I draw back, her eyes are on my face, searching for a sign that I can feel it too, the thin wire of need stretched tight between us.

And yeah, fuck yeah, I can feel it. I can feel it across the surface of my skin and buried deep in my flesh and throbbing through my veins. My cock, flush now, strains against my hiking shorts.

"That's okay. You don't have to say it. I know you're still pretending you aren't turned on. But I know you are. I can see it. I can see it here—" I lightly run my thumb over the flush on her cheeks—"and here—" I touch her lower lip, soft with need— "and here—" I brush my fingertips across the pink on the upper curves of her breasts— "and here—" I drop a hand so my palm barely scrapes the sensitive tip of those hard nipples, and she gasps involuntarily, her eyes flying to mine.

I grin.

She frowns so deeply it looks like it hurts.

"You're probably wet, too, but I won't make you admit that, not yet."

She crosses her arms, hiding her nipples from my appreciative gaze.

My grin gets bigger. "Even if I weren't looking at you, I could tell you're turned on."

She throws her arms out, exasperated. "That's just bullshit."

"Yeah? Okay. Close your eyes."

I watch as she does, eyes falling shut. Her long lashes are charcoal-black, her skin still fair despite her midsummer tan. "Snow White," I murmur, not quite meaning to, but even though this is my game and I'm in charge, I'm rapidly learning that I'm never completely in charge when it comes to Hanna.

"What?"

"Nothing. Listen," I say. "Hear your breathing?"

We listen together, her breath rapid and needy, then slowing a little as she gets it more under control.

"And you smell so fucking good, Han. So fucking good. I don't know flowers, but I feel like I'm walking in a garden." Her breath speeds again, and I push my luck. "By the sea," I add.

She makes a choking sound. "Did you just—?"

I open my eyes to find her outraged and also trying not to laugh.

"Oh, yeah, I did," I say. I put a finger in the middle of her chest, above the neckline of her tank top, and I run it down into her cleavage, over the curve of her belly, to the V of her pussy. "You smell so good *right fucking here*. If you let me lick you, I know you're going to taste so good, too."

Her breath catches. No mistaking it. I raise my eyebrows, and she rolls her eyes.

I'm so hard it hurts, but there's no way I'm going to stop this game, not until I win it.

And I'll know when I have.

"Lie back," I tell her.

She narrows her eyes at me. "Will you claim victory if I do?"

"I told you, Han, you'll know when you lose this fight."

I put my hands on her hips. She unfolds her legs and I ease her down onto the sleeping bag, lowering myself next to her. I want to be on top of her, but I need her to want it more.

I tug one tank top strap off her shoulder, then jerk the fabric lower to expose her breast. I draw her nipple into my mouth and tongue it, feeling her body tremble and twitch under me. Then I slide down the other strap and tend to the other breast. She's panting now.

I ease her tank top down her torso.

"Lift up," I say, and work her top over her hips and ass, her delectable thighs, her curvy calves, and off. On my way down, I bury my face between her legs and take a deep breath, full of her salty scent. Her thighs twitch like they're aching to squeeze together.

"You can if you need to," I tell her. "If you want to squeeze those gorgeous thighs together, you can."

"Fuck you, Easton," she says roughly, like she's hanging onto the last shred of her control. "Fuck you."

"Do you want me to?"

She's quiet.

"You don't have to say it, Han. I know it." I set my palm over the perfect triangle of her mound, and press, working the pressure around until I find the spot that makes her arch and push back. I give her friction, pressure, and when she jerks her hips hungrily, I cup her tight through her hiking shorts and tug on her flesh, kneading her sensitive outer lips.

A moan escapes her.

"What? What was that? You like it? You want more?"

"I hate you," she says.

"I know," I say. "Tell me how much. Tell me how much you hate me." I trail kisses from her breasts, over the silky skin of her belly. When I reach the fasteners for her shorts, I unsnap and unzip her. "Lift up," I say again, and she does, and I slide her shorts down and confront the reality of her in nothing but a pair of black cotton boy shorts.

So fucking hot. I stare at her for a few moments, unable to believe my luck, unable to look my fill.

"What?" she asks, and despite my own all-consuming hunger, I catch the uncertainty in her voice.

"You're the prettiest thing I've ever seen."

"You're full of shit," she says.

"No," I tell her. "I've seen a lot. But I've never seen anything as pretty as you, Han."

"I wish you wouldn't—"

She sounds flustered and frustrated, so much so that my impulse is to apologize, but I don't. I ease her underpants down and find an unexpected surprise. Her pussy is bare. It's so completely at odds with Hanna's uncompromising practicality.

"Whoa."

"I do it for myself," she says stubbornly. "I like the way it feels."

"You—"

She's rendered me speechless, with her pretty bare pussy and the words she's just said.

"The way it—" I repeat, dumbly. And then, because I need to know, I stroke a finger over her bare lips.

They're the softest thing I've ever felt. Soft as velvet, as flower petals.

"Fuck, Hanna," I curse, and that's when my self-control cracks. I fall on her, my mouth sealing over her seam, my tongue seeking her clit, my hands reaching up to tweak and twist and pinch her nipples.

My tongue finds its goal, her clit swollen, pushing out from its hood and reaching for me. "Tell me," I demand, lifting my face just long enough to say it. "Tell me what you want. Exactly what you want."

Because I know she knows. And we're done playing games.

"Your fingers in me," she says. "And suck."

I slide two fingers into her, her wet core already clenching around me, her clit starting to spasm against the onslaught of my tongue, and it's just another second of that, of Hanna all over and around me, before she's coming, crying my name.

I ease myself up on one elbow, wiping my face with the back of my hand, grinning at her.

"There," I say. "Told you you'd know when you'd lost."

It takes her a moment. She raises her head first, her eyes sleepy and satisfied, which makes me feel like I won something incalculably valuable. Then she grins.

"You think I lost?" She laughs. "Whatever that game was, I *definitely* won."

31

HANNA

on't go online.

The first message, a few days after the camping trip, is from Lucy, but it's followed by messages from Rachel, Jessa, Mari, Kane, Barb, Geneva, and even my brother Shane.

Oh, shit.

So, what do I do?

I go online, of course.

Human nature, man; it sucks. It sucks to the tune of hundreds of Instagram notifications and quite a few DMs.

Bear posted a video.

I don't think he *meant* to be a total and complete dick, but... well, he's managed it anyway.

In the video, he's sitting by himself by the campfire. The camera is stationary, as if it's on a stand, so I'm guessing Cypress had gone to bed. It must have been recorded after Easton and I crept back to the tent together.

He's drinking from a flask, which he raises to the viewer.

"Single malt scotch," he says. "Oban. Extra peaty. Good for pity parties."

Because of the volume of comments and DMs, because of my friends' messages, I'm pretty sure I know where this is going, but my stomach *still* drops like I'm in a faulty elevator.

"Tough week, guys. Hanna told me she's not interested in taking things further."

Giving him the maximum benefit of the doubt, he must have felt he had to let his viewers know he and I weren't going to be a thing, and thought this would be a good way to do it.

But holy *shit*, if he didn't foresee what would happen next, he's either an idiot or an asshole.

Right now, I'm voting for both.

Bear carries on with a sorrowful bite of his lip. "And I'm just super bummed out about it. You know when you meet someone who just feels so perfect for you?"

He gives the camera a woeful glance. "I mean, she's cute, she's smart, she's at home in the woods, and she loves to eat even more than I do. I know I'll get over this, but... it just hurts right now, not gonna lie. So, if you're out there, having a tough night, too, just know I feel you."

And he signs off, with another wry, sad smile, and tip of his flask.

I can only imagine how many women just slid into his DMs to tell him they feel his pain.

Meanwhile, in the comments... and in my DMs...

Oh, shit.

Well, you know the drill. I won't recap. His viewers pick

on my pixie haircut and weight, they hate on my fashion choices, and they berate me for thinking I can do better than Bear, when Bear is so obviously waaaay above my pay grade.

Don't pay any attention to them.

Stop reading!

Stop... stop... stop.

But I can't look away. It's the sickest form of FOMO, not wanting the rest of the world to know what's being said about me if I don't.

Even if I really, really don't want to know.

I read until I can't breathe and my eyes burn, and then I throw my phone down on the couch. I wedge my feet into my sneakers and let the front door shut behind me. There's only one place I want to go when I feel like this, and that's down to the edge of the river that runs along our property line.

It's where I've always gone when things are tough, where I went the day of my mom's funeral when I had to get away from all the people and their concern and questions. It's where I ran when my brothers teased and taunted and pushed me to the outside of their impenetrable boy circle, and when the girls in school teased and taunted and pushed me to the outside of their closed girl world.

And today, it's where I go to escape my ugly fifteen minutes of unearned, unwanted fame, since I'm definitely *not* an Internet "it" girl. I'm an Internet "out" girl.

I don't want to give a shit. About any of it. I've spent my life learning how not to give a shit.

I'm a pro by now.

I bend, pick up a stone, skip it.

The water's high this year—lots of snow melt—very different from the drought year when my mother died. With the water rushing, it's hard to see what happens to the stone, how many times it bounces before it sinks.

I'm not sure how long I stand there, skipping stones, trying to trace their trajectory across the surface, feeling my heartbeat slowly ease back to normal, before I hear foot-steps behind me. I don't have to look to know it's Easton; he's the only one who'd look for me down here. He comes up beside me. Squats.

"Don't," I say.

"Don't what?"

"Don't give me a stone. I'll just brain you with it."

A small laugh huffs out of him. Just the sound of it makes me feel a little better.

He does it anyway, searching in the dirt for one he likes and pressing it into my palm. I rub my fingers over it, testing it; it's the perfect worry stone. I slide it into my pocket and hold out my hand for another.

"What, doesn't meet your standards?"

I don't tell him it's too perfect to skip. I just shake my hand impatiently until he presses another stone into it. I release it and watch it skid and bounce over the water's surface.

He picks one up and skips it so it follows a few steps behind mine—before they both disappear under the surface.

We do it for a few more minutes, until the sting slowly starts to go out of all those strangers' words.

The feel of him next to me is safety and belonging.

I want to tell him that, but I can't imagine doing so, because even hearing the words in my head is scary. Like by thinking them I've made them true, and by making them true, I've dared the universe to take them away from me.

After a while, she heaves a big sigh. Like it's the first time she's been able to really breathe, but also like all the fight's finally gone out of her. Even so, I don't ask if she's okay. I know she doesn't know the answer and wouldn't want to tell me even if she did. What she wants, what she needs, is for me to just... be here.

"People are mean." Her voice is angry, a punch back at the haters, but also etched with hurt.

"They sure can be."

She still doesn't look at me. She stares out at the lake as she says, "I got a lot of texts from your brothers' girlfriends and your sister. Telling me not to go online. Warning me. It was super nice of them."

"They're your friends, Hanna. They'd go to the mat for you."

"Would they?"

"Of course they would!"

She presses her lips together.

"If you don't believe that, you definitely don't know Amanda. Or Lucy. Or any of them." I gesture to the two of us. "What do they have to say about all this? About us?"

"I haven't told them."

"Nothing? Not even about the kissing lessons?"

"You know how they are. They'll want to make it into a thing. Talk about feelings. And besides. What would I tell them? 'Your brother's helping me break my sex drought?'"

She hugs herself, rocking, as if chilly. I reach out and draw her against me, close to my side, and she stiffens for a moment and then lets out another long exhale. It reminds me, heartbreakingly, of the way babies sigh just before they relax completely, seeping body heat and falling into sleep with utter trust.

"I'm your dirty secret?" I tease.

"You're the best dirty secret," she says, smiling for the first time.

"Does that mean we're going to pretend nothing's going on at family dinner?" There's a friends-and-family dinner going down at Gabe's house tomorrow night.

She tilts her head. "I think we have to, right?"

"You really think we'll be able to pull that off?"

"What would give us away?"

"Maybe the fact that I can't keep my eyes or my hands off you?" I ask, stroking a hand over her arm, brushing the side of her breast accidentally on purpose as I do so.

"For a couple of hours you can, right?"

"Yes," I say. "For a couple of hours, no prob. Then after that, you're all mine, and I'm going to make up for lost time."

She makes a soft purring sound I feel in my cock.

"Hey," I say. "I got you something. And it's not a rock."

"Is that a dirty come-on line?"

"For once? It's not. I bought you something."

She perks up. "Yeah? What is it?"

"Come back to my place. I'll show you."

WHEN WE GET BACK to my apartment—caravanning with her truck behind my car—I go into the bedroom and come back out with a paper bag, folded over several times. And suddenly I'm self-conscious. Suddenly, what seemed like a great idea when I first had it seems...

All wrong.

"Maybe this was a bad idea," I say, drawing the bag to my body.

She cocks her head. "Are you taking the gift back before you even give it to me?"

"I'm just. Okay, I think I need to explain this. Because it made sense in my head, but it's not going to make sense to you. I don't think."

Her mouth is curved, like she's trying not to smile, which might be my second favorite look on her, after the scowl she can't *quite* keep on her face.

"So maybe I'm wrong about this..."

I stop. Why is this so hard?

"I guess I had this feeling that..."

"Easton," she says, exasperated. "Just *say* it."

"I know you say you don't like 'girly' things. And I know that's true. But I also know you said you liked that Bear Warden knew how to treat a woman. I could tell you liked the idea that he wanted to take you to a fancy restaurant and treat you—I don't know, like a *girl*. And I've never treated you like a girl. I guess... I wanted, just for a minute, to do that. Treat you like a girl."

I wait for her to shake her head. Tell me I'm nuts. But that's not what happens. She blushes, actually. And bites her bottom lip.

"I'm not wrong, then?" I ask.

"You're not wrong," she whispers. And then, shocking me, her voice so low I can barely hear her, "I thought it might be nice for once. To be treated like a princess."

"Yeah. That's how I wanted you to feel. Like a princess."

She gives me a sharp look, like she's trying to suss out if I could be making fun of her, but I think she can see how serious I am. And her eyes go soft and uncertain.

Except now I'm really not sure if I've fucked this up beyond all recognition. But it's too late now; I have to explain myself. "Okay, so... well, here's the thing. I went shopping. By myself. And I picked out a lot of beautiful things. Things that would look amazing on you, by the way. I was thinking about you wearing all these beautiful things, and hard the whole time, picturing it."

She gets pinker.

"Worst way to shop, honestly." I shake my head. "But then, I don't know, I was standing in the lingerie shop with all this stuff, and it didn't feel quite right. Like I was buying you a costume. Instead of... instead of clothes. If that makes sense? So, I put it all back and..."

I thrust the bag into her hands. "I guess... I'm not sure if this is what a princess would wear. But it felt like... it felt like what *you'd* wear."

The white of her tooth digs into the red of her lower lip, and all I can think about is how much I want to lick that lip, lick into her mouth, lick her all over.

She unfolds the bag and reaches in. Pulls out the two things I bought her. Lingerie, I guess. If you want to call it that.

"Oh," she says, and for a second I'm sure I've gotten it all wrong. I reach my hand out, like I'm going to snatch it back, like I can undo how wrong I've read her. So I can run back to the mall and grab the lacy pink nightgown or the seafoam green bra-and-thong set. So I can make her feel like she wanted Bear to make her feel.

Like a princess.

But she won't let me. She holds them out of reach, then sets the two items on the bed and stares down at them.

She turns to me. Her eyes are so bright. Soft.

She's Hanna, so all she says is, "I'm going to put them on now."

That's how I know I did okay.

33

———————

HANNA

I go into the bathroom and change. I spend a long time looking at myself in the mirror, feeling like…

Like me.

I'm wearing a pair of plain but very cheeky black boy shorts, cut from the softest cottony fabric you can possibly imagine.

And a cropped, snug t-shirt that says, in letters that swerve across my chest:

Not fragile like a flower. Fragile like a bomb.

"Hell yes," he says, when I come out. "Fuck yes."

I can't hold back my smile. It's busting out all over the place, like my boobs in this shirt, like my ass in these shorts. And from the look on Easton's face, he wholeheartedly approves.

It's the best fucking thing, the way he's looking at me; I could eat it for every meal the rest of my life.

And I think, with a burst of joy and a spasm of fear, intertwined like vines, that maybe I never wanted to be anyone's princess. I just wanted to be Easton's Hanna.

"Hanna," he says, and he strides toward me, takes me in his arms and kisses me.

No messing around with this kiss. He's hungry and bossy, his hands already all over my body—on the boy shorts, on my ass, at my waist, on my breasts. He's greedy and giving by turns—devouring my mouth, slicking my tongue with his, clutching my curves—and then teasing along the seam of my lips, finding my nipple with two talented and determined fingers, stroking a featherlight hand down over my mound and pressing just for a second to give me a zap of pleasure.

Not sure how we got there, but we're on our knees, now, unable to stop kissing, moaning into each other's mouths.

"Take them off," he commands, tugging at my new t-shirt.

"I just put them on."

"Take them off."

"You take yours off!"

"I will if you do."

I'm surprised neither of us tears anything, given the haste with which we lose our clothes.

"Oh, Jesus, Easton," I say. "You're—"

He's beautiful. Hard muscle, thick through shoulders and chest, ridged down his belly. A just-right smattering of golden hair on his pecs, and a line of darker hair that starts under his navel and dives toward his jutting cock.

Like the rest of him, his cock is pretty. Perfect. Thick and well-formed, the head shiny with how hard he is. For me. He's that hard *for me*.

"Just hold still for a minute," I say, and I reach a hand out.

He groans as my fingers touch the bare skin of his arms, his shoulders, his chest, his abs. I want to feel the solidness and the give, the smoothness of his bare skin and the just-rough-enough feel of his body hair.

"This is the fantasy I never let myself have," I admit. "Getting to touch the pretty."

He snorts laughter, but I'm dead serious. "You don't understand, Easton. I've only ever had sex with mortal men."

Now he's really laughing.

My hand slides down over the ridges of his abs and finds his cock, and he stops laughing.

"I'm going to have this inside me," I say conversationally, fisting him. And then because turnabout is fair play, "Tell me what you want. Exactly what you want."

"Your mouth," he says without hesitation, then, "if that's okay?"

I burst out laughing. "Alpha with a side of twenty-first century consent."

"I mean," he says, "it's where we are."

"And on that note, before I suck your cock—"

"Hanna..."

"Health status report required," I say.

"Whiplash," he says, laughing. Then he sobers up. "Doctor's visit a month ago, all clear, nothing since."

I raise my eyebrows.

"If we're being honest, not all that much for a while before that, either. For, I don't know, getting on towards a year."

"*Really.*"

"Really and truly."

"Why?"

He looks away from me for a split second, then back, and his eyes hold mine. "It wasn't working for me."

"What wasn't?"

"Having sex with anyone who gave me attention."

"Then why'd you do it?"

"It just happened," he says. "I was good at it. And you know how it is in a big family. Everyone kind of gets their role, and people latch onto it. Maybe so they can tell you apart. Boss, bad boy, whatever. In my case, good-times brother."

I feel a small, sharp stab somewhere in my chest as Easton slips into sharp relief. The man I thought I knew—who flirted with and probably fucked anything that moved—becomes something else. Someone else.

"Not so easy being the youngest Wilder, huh?" I ask.

"Not so easy being the youngest Hott, either," he says.

It's not a question.

We look at each other for a long time, and even though he is a thing of beauty and it's very tempting to stare at his body, I discover I don't want to look away from the tenderness in his eyes.

"I guess that's part of why we like each other, huh?"

"Part of it," he says. "Not all of it."

"So how does this fit in? Sex with me?"

He closes his eyes. His face is both so pretty and so masculine; it's impossible for me to look away, or not to want to kiss his lush mouth and touch the hard, honed jaw. But I leave him alone for the moment because I want his answer more.

He opens his eyes. "I realized…" He hesitates. "I realized

it's better with someone you like. Someone who makes you laugh. Someone who... who knows you."

"Yeah?"

"Yeah." He touches the curve of my cheek, then runs a palm down the front of my throat, dropping it down to cup my breast and toy with my nipple.

"Mmm," I say. "Keep doing that while I..." I drop to all fours, bringing my mouth within a whisper of his cock.

"Hang on," he says.

He grabs a throw blanket from the arm of a nearby chair and spreads it on the carpet, then tugs me down.

I slide along his body, taking the head of his cock in my mouth. I explore with my tongue, warming both of us up.

He makes an incoherent sound I love.

I swirl my tongue, caress the head of his cock, suck up and down his length, until his breath is short and raspy. He's shiny-hard in my mouth, and I know he's not going to last. And then I stroke his balls and urge him to just come for me. Let go.

Which he does, calling my name and coming in spurts against my tongue.

"You should have told me how good you were at that," he says breathlessly, when I ease myself back up his body and lay my head on his (perfect) chest.

"Because what?" I ask. "You would have suggested we do this sooner?"

"Yeah."

I don't point out how that never would have happened. I'm not sure exactly what alchemy led to us being together like this, but I know it's a brew of Bear's interest in me and him knowing he's leaving anyway. Jealousy on one hand and nothing to lose on the other.

"Give me a minute to catch my breath," he says. "Then it's your turn."

I rest my head against the thrum of his heart, in no rush for this moment to end. Right now is perfect, and the future is... complicated.

But Easton's as good as his word. As soon as his breath eases back to normal, he rolls me onto my back and props himself on one elbow, looking down at me. His other hand slowly explores the contours of my body—face, throat, breasts, belly, thighs, then back up again to settle between my legs. The weight of his hand heavy on the softest part of my sex, his fingers idly, almost innocently, teasing between my folds. After a moment, it's just one finger, which he dips to my core, then brings back up to my clit, slick and light. So light that at first, I want to tell him it won't work, it's not enough, but as I open my mouth, the protest dies away. That one finger, a slow, silky, brush, back and forth, with infinite patience. The tension builds from nowhere, becomes a rush of heat, a fierce burn, and then, Easton magic, yanks everything taut in my pelvis, my belly, my thighs, and I'm coming, whimpering, burying my face in his neck and crying his name.

34

HANNA

We haul ourselves and the blanket up onto the couch. We cuddle there until Easton recovers enough to re-don his boxer briefs and go in search of food and drink. I get up, retrieve my own newly acquired "clothes," and turn on Netflix.

He walks back into the room just as the TV flicks to life, on a freeze frame of Kate Sharma fleeing the Bridgertons' gardens after—

"What!?" I cry.

Easton drops our food on the table, grabs the remote out of my hand, and quickly flicks up through the menu system until the incriminating evidence disappears.

"Easton Wilder, were you watching *Bridgerton* season *two*?"

"I plead the fifth!" he says.

"Did you pause after the bee scene?!"

"I have the right to an attorney! At least give me my phone call."

"You were! You did! You watched it, and you paused

after the bee scene!" I get up and cross to him, grabbing his arms and shaking him. "Admit it!"

"I have a right to a fair trial! With a jury of my peers!"

"I am your peers!"

Laughing, he takes my head in his hands, lowers his mouth to mine, and presses a kiss to my lips. Then drops his arms and hugs me tight, nearly lifting me off the ground, swaying me back and forth, his cheek pressed to mine. "Hanna," he says. "God. I—"

He stops. Then starts again. "I have so much fun with you," he says, but there's something in his voice, something too somber for his words, and I wonder if that's what he meant to say.

"I have fun with you, too," I say into his chest, "But you're not getting off the hook that easily! Confess, and I'll go easy on you. You can plead guilty and avoid *so* much nastiness."

He hugs me again, then releases me. "Okay. Yes. I watched *Bridgerton*, and when I finished that episode, I watched the bee scene again. But not because it was fucking sexy or I was planning to do anything X-rated while I rewatched. No. Definitely not."

"You. Did. Not. Jerk. Off. To. The. Bee. Scene."

Easton is trying very hard not to laugh. "As it happens, I did not... although only because my phone rang right at that extremely inopportune moment and it was, even more inopportunely, my mother saying that she and Geneva had ordered too much Indian food, and did I want some?"

"Oh my *God*, your *mom* cock-blocked you from jerking off to the bee scene? It's like a *Bridgerton* episode! It's like a

Bridgerton episode inside a *Bridgerton* episode, all the way to infinity!"

He's laughing in earnest now.

"Does this mean you watched all of season one, too?"

At this, he swallows hard. I've known Easton a long, long time—and more to the point, I have lots of experience with trouble-making boys—and I know guilt when I see it. "Mmm. Yes. I did."

"Why?"

"What do you mean, *why*? Why does anyone watch *Bridgerton*? To see beautiful people in colorful period costumes getting it on, right?"

"Really? Really and truly?"

"What are you getting at, Hanna Hott?"

"If you know, you know," I say mysteriously.

Easton's cheeks turn a lovely shade of pink. "I may or may not have watched the first season of *Bridgerton* after you praised the Duke of Hastings' ass in that one RV redesign meeting."

"Ha!" I say, pointing a finger. "I *knew* it!"

"And I may or may not have spent an exceptionally long time craning to see my own ass in the mirror, in an effort to ascertain—ass-ertain!—" he crows, making himself laugh. "—whether mine would pass muster in a comparative study."

"Wait," I say. "Because?"

"Because I wanted to know if my ass would meet your high standards," he admits.

"Noooo," I say. "That is *not* a thing!"

I am delighted, though. Even if he's just kidding around, the idea of Easton Wilder, hottest guy I know, giving more than a passing thought to whether I would find his ass up to snuff…

It's just too awesome.

"Well," I say. "You'll have to let me judge. We'll do a head-to-head—er, no, rear-to-rear comparison." I grab the remote back, with every intention of calling up the assiest Duke scene I can find in season one—or at least making him think I'm going to, which is good enough.

He howls and collapses on the couch beside me, hiding the ass in question. That's okay; I know from having had my hands all over it a few minutes ago, it *will* pass muster, even in a rear-to-rear comparison with the Duke of Hastings.

I turn my attention to the food on the coffee table instead. "What'd you bring us?"

"A bag of cheddar popcorn, two cartons of Ben and Jerry's, and a couple of beers."

I hoot my approval and grab a carton and a spoon. Half-baked. He takes the other cartoon, mint Oreo cookie.

"Eat up," he says. "You're going to need your energy, because I'm not done with you."

My tongue is already registering the cool creaminess of my ice cream, but the rest of my body flushes warm at his words.

It's not a bad combo.

"If someone had told you a week and a half ago we'd be eating ice cream together, from the carton, in our under-wear—" I raise my spoon in inquiry.

"I would have asked them what they were smoking."

"Yeah," I agree.

But here's the thing: It doesn't feel weird *at all*.

35

HANNA

The next afternoon, I go on a Bear hunt. It's not as hard you might expect. I have Cypress's phone number.

"Where is he?" I demand, when Bear's assistant answers.

They sigh. "Are you going to hurt him?"

So they already know about the video and the comments. "What if I say yes?"

"Then I would say, 'You have my blessing' and tell you that he's at Oscar's."

That startles a laugh out of me.

"I hope you know that if I'd seen that video before he posted it, I would have stopped him."

I absorb that. "Hey. Thanks. And, uh… I won't tell him you sent me."

They snort. "Oh, feel free. I already told him what I thought of whiskey-fueled late-night confessions and him asking me to film his dates. He hired me to film a cooking show, not the dating game."

My turn to snort. "How'd he take that?"

"Surprisingly well. He's a hot-head, not an asshole, recent events notwithstanding."

"Well. I'm glad you still have your job."

"Me, too," they say. "And I'm glad you and I get to work together for a few more weeks."

"Even though your plant babies are at the mercy of your room-monster?"

"Would you believe it? The babies are hanging in. I might have a garden this year after all."

"And a roommate," I tease.

"And a roommate," they agree.

I thank them for being generally awesome and hang up.

I FIND Bear at the bar at Oscar's drinking—yes—peaty Scotch.

I slide in next to him, take the glass out of his hand, down the rest of his liquor, and say, "That video? Was a completely dickish thing to do."

"I know."

Startled, I almost fall off my seat.

"I'm really, really sorry," he says.

To my surprise, he sounds like he means it. And, when I turn to face him, he *looks* like he means it. And not in a for-the-cameras way.

Just to be sure, I peek around—but there's no one filming us.

He slides his Oscar's coaster back and forth on the

glossy surface of the bar. "I didn't think—I wasn't expecting my viewers to go after you like that."

"Seriously? What did you *think* was going to happen?" I demand.

He flips the coaster over, then back, not meeting my eyes. "I guess I thought... I thought people would... not... suck so much."

I roll my eyes. "You mean to tell me that the master of the Internet hasn't learned yet that if there's the chance for a pile on, people will take it? Don't bullshit me."

He hangs his head. "If it helps at all, I took the video down. And I put this up." He takes his phone out of his pocket, unlocks it, and hands it to me.

The new video is short. To the point. A full apology, a dressing down of his viewers for their behavior, a promise to do better from now on, and a request that they do the same.

When I'm done watching, I hand him back the phone and say, "Well, that's something."

"I wish I could just... undo it." He repockets his phone.

I grimace. "Yeah, there's no undo button. And you're really fucking lucky no one showed up on my doorstep."

I don't tell him that if they had, I wouldn't have known about it, because I was at Easton's place, having ice cream licked off my body.

The memory goes a long way towards improving my mood, I have to admit. I feel almost capable of forgiveness.

"I'm really sorry, Han," Bear says again.

"Whatever," I say. "People have short memories. I'll be fine. Just don't ever fucking do something like that again. To me or anyone else. It's brutal out there, especially for women." I raise my eyebrows. "You do know that, right?"

He sighs.

"Don't do it again."

"Swear I won't," Bear says.

"You're lucky I don't hold grudges," I inform him.

The bartender, a woman I know slightly, approaches. "Hey, Han! How goes it?"

"Hey, Janie. It's been a challenging couple of days, but I think I'm on the upswing. You?"

"Ah, you know. Another day in paradise. Spent yesterday hiking, so can't complain. Bear, another Lagavulin?"

"Yes, please," he says.

"Han?"

"Same."

As she retreats, Bear turns to me again. "You know, you're not the first person today to tell me I'm a dick?"

"Good," I say.

"I thought you didn't hold grudges."

"This is me, not holding a grudge."

The corner of his mouth turns up.

I raise my eyebrows. "Who else called you a dick today?"

"Easton showed up at my Airbnb this morning, told me there was no way he could work for a guy who would let his viewers pile on anyone like that, and said I owed you a real apology." His mouth flattens wryly.

I try to hold back my smile but can't.

"He was *pissed,*" Bear says. He crosses his arms and eyes me. "Hanna?"

"Yeah?"

"Can I ask you something?"

"Sure."

"You and Easton? What's the story there?"

I can feel myself turning bright red, and I guess my blush is answer enough, because Bear's eyebrows go way up. "Easton said there wasn't anything going on, but I should have known," he grumbles.

Oh, shit.

As much as I don't want Easton to go to Colorado, I don't want to be the thing that ruins his chances, either.

"He didn't lie to you on purpose," I say quickly. "We weren't—it wasn't like this when you asked him. He didn't realize that things between him and me were going to get so..."

Combustible.

Irresistible.

Good-sense flattening.

So. Fucking. Hot.

My face is getting redder, which probably won't help things. "Complicated," I finish. "Just, please—give him another chance. He's a good guy, and he'd be great for the job."

Bear tilts his head. "Wait. Are you arguing for the guy you're dating to move to Colorado?"

I close my eyes, trying not to imagine Easton in Golden, Colorado—or really, Rush Creek without Easton.

I open them again, to find Bear watching me, brow furrowed. I sigh. "It's not that I want him to move to Colorado. I just want him to be..."

Damn it. I know the fact that this sentence is coming out of my mouth means I've lost control of the situation.

"...happy."

Bear's eyebrows go up.

"Don't," I say. "Just, don't. Whatever you're going to say, don't say it."

"I was just going to say, you really like this guy."

He went and said it, damn him. And it's true. It's so fucking true, and I'm so screwed, and...

Right now, I don't even care.

Bear nods. "I'm not going to hold this against him," he says. "I wish he hadn't lied to me, but I get that he didn't mean to. I know how these things can just... happen. And I like his work. He's a genius with video editing, he looks good on camera, he and I get along well, and I think we can negotiate around each other's egos."

I hide a smile. I don't envy either of them that part of the job.

"Plus, to be honest, it's good to know this"—he gestures between the two of us— "isn't about me. Helps with the rejection to know the *why*."

"Anything to soothe that ego."

He smiles wryly at me. And I can't help myself, I have to add:

"As for the *why*? Pro tip? Maybe, if you really like a woman? Don't wait to kiss her till the camera's running."

He winces. "Yeah. Noted. I think sometimes I... forget that there's a life off camera."

"I can see how that would happen," I say, for the first time feeling a tiny bit sorry for Bear. Fame is... double-edged. "Though in fairness, even if you had kissed me off camera, it probably wouldn't have helped."

Bear sighs. "I never stood a chance, did I."

It's really not a question, so I don't bother answering it.

"Bear?" I ask, instead.

"Yeah?"

"Can you maybe not say anything about me and Easton to... well, anyone?"

"Gabe doesn't know, huh?" he asks, the corner of his mouth turning up.

"No one knows," I admit.

He raises an eyebrow. "Except, you, Easton, me, and... well, pretty much everyone else in Oscar's right now."

My mouth falls open again.

"Just kidding," he says. "But I've only been in Rush Creek a few weeks, and I already know it *could* be true."

"You go in first," Hanna says. She's standing stock still next to her truck, eyeing Gabe's house warily, like it might bite.

We're standing in the Wilder headquarters parking lot, having arrived in separate vehicles, but moments apart. We didn't plan it; it just happened.

"We could walk in together," I say. "Like we would normally if we arrived at the same time."

"But this isn't *normally*," Hanna says. "The other night wasn't *normal*."

"Which part?" I tease her. "The part where you blew me on a blanket on my living room floor? The part where I made you yell my name with one finger? Or the part where we ate Ben & Jerry's mostly naked and then I spread ice cream on your nip—"

"Shh!" She looks around wildly.

"Maybe we should just tell them," I suggest. "Then you don't have to worry about me being overheard when I wax rhapsodic about licking ice cream off you."

She smacks me, hard, in the arm. "Shut *up*. Keep it simple, stupid. Take my word for it, when you're done with me, you'll be glad they're not all up in our business."

There she goes again, already writing an ending for us. "I'm not planning to be done with you any time soo—"

"Hey!"

We turn, a coordinated dance move, to find Amanda rapidly approaching from the house. "Quit arguing in the parking lot and come see Zara walking!"

"I'm not ready to think about this ending," I tell her quietly, as we hurry behind Amanda.

She gives me a startled glance, and there's vulnerability in her expression. A softness, a hopefulness, that sets off an answering echo in my chest. She opens her mouth, like she's about to speak, but just then, Amanda looks back at us, and the soft expression slides right off Hanna's face, replaced with something aloof and slightly mischievous.

And I realize: the Hanna I spar with in public—that's a mask she wears. The real Hanna is the one down at the riverbank, the one chucking rocks into the water. The one turning pink because I bought her a gift, the one whose eyes went bright when the gift was for her and not just for the generic woman she was afraid she was to me.

I want to reach out and clutch her hand. I want to claim her in front of my sister and the rest of my family—in front of God, for that matter. But I know, because she's put the mask back on, that she doesn't trust me enough yet for that. And I can't say I blame her. I don't trust me. I don't know what I'm doing or what I want from her or whether I have any right to ask it, given that a couple of weeks ago I was still thinking about sex in terms of ice cream flavors.

So, when Amanda turns away again, I content myself with giving Hanna's shoulder a nudge with mine.

And if I'm disappointed that the glance she gives me is the mischievous one, the one that promises earthly delights later, and not the one filled with shy hope, I shut that disappointment down and content myself with what I've got.

Turns out it's not that easy to keep your hands and eyes off someone you're crazy about.

I accidentally intercept Hanna as I'm heading for the washroom and she's coming out. She's wearing the outfit from the first shopping trip. The body-hugging leggings and tank, and the drapey top thing—except she's taken off the drapey top thing.

"Where's your—sweatshirt-y thing?" I say, demonstrating my deep knowledge of women's fashion.

"I took it off because if I'm not careful the long back part ends up in the toilet."

I snort.

"That doesn't happen when I wear tees and sweatshirts and hiking pants," she grumbles, sweeping past me toward the kitchen.

I turn to follow her with my eyes, not bothering to be subtle about it because it's just the two of us. She is all visible, scrumptious curves, and— "Are you not wearing any underwear?" I demand.

She smirks at me over her shoulder.

I grab her arm, turning her back towards me, tugging her closer. "Did you just smirk at me?"

"Possibly," she says, freeing herself and teasingly backing away.

This brings up another important question. "Were you not wearing any underwear at work that day when Bear was there for the first trip debrief?"

"Were you looking at my ass that day?" Hanna asks innocently. "Were you looking at my ass just now?"

"You know I was," I growl, reaching for it.

She darts out of my grasp and giggles. It is one of the best sounds I have ever heard. I want to make her laugh like a high school girl. I want to make her giggle, and also belly laugh and chuckle and roll her eyes at me and scowl and...

"Answer the question," I say, stalking toward her. She takes a step back, but the expression on her face is still school-girl pleased.

I back her up against the wall, then take another step, bringing our bodies together. The collision of her hip with my already-eager cock makes both of us groan. I tuck my hand into the back of her leggings and find the tiny triangle of fabric at the dimpled curve of her ass. "Thong," I whisper.

Footsteps approach, and we jump apart. Jessa and Clark come down the hallway, take stock of us, and... grin.

"Did we interrupt something?" Jessa asks slyly.

I have a split second of desperately wanting to say *Yes, and please go away so we can pick up where we left off*, before Hanna says, "Just another fight."

Jessa looks disappointed. "What was it this time?" she asks.

Hanna's expression goes panicky.

"Hanna thinks we should... do a pizza-in-the-woods

series using the Bear model. And I was explaining that the crust would be a nightmare. Imagine trying to clean flour and goopy dough off everything with a water bottle and leave-no-trace sink."

Hanna raises her eyebrows, clearly impressed at my improv skills.

"Have to admit, I'm gonna vote with Easton on this one," Clark says. The two of them continue on down the hall, leaving us alone again.

"That was impressive," Hanna says. "Your bullshitting skills are legendary." She doesn't sound mad, but in some ways that's worse. The mask is back on.

I know what she's thinking. That if I could lie that nimbly to Jessa and Clark, maybe I've done it to her, too. "I don't bullshit you, Hanna," I tell her.

"I know you don't," she says, her voice gentling a bit.

I dip my head and press my mouth to hers. There's a moment's hesitation and then she opens to me, whimpering.

She draws back first. "We got away with it this time, but we probably shouldn't push our luck, huh?"

"I want to push my luck so hard with you, Han," I murmur against her hair, and am rewarded with her chuckle.

"Easton," Gabe says sharply.

"Sorry, what?"

"Where's your head? You were staring into space."

Actually, that's not true. I was staring out into the yard,

where Hanna is playing a game of flag football with my brothers, a few of the girlfriends and wives, and my nieces and nephews.

Hanna is, on top of all her other excellent traits, a really good athlete. Quick-footed and a fast runner—as you would expect from a former college rugby captain—and...

And even though I've watched her run across Gabe's backyard a hundred times before, it has never looked as tempting as it looks right now.

"I was... thinking about..."

I've really got nothing. Like, nothing.

Which Gabe can clearly sense. He says, "Never mind. Not fair of me to ask you a work question at a party."

"That's never stopped you before," I point out.

"True," he admits. "But Lucy has informed me that I need to break that habit."

"Lucy is a good influence."

"She is," he says fondly, and then it's his turn to follow his wife with his eyes as she runs down the field.

"I don't mind, though," I say. "Hit me."

"I just wanted a download on what you think about the Bear workshops. Whether something like that could work for us. And I'm curious to know if you're learning some stuff that could be useful for the business. I liked the TikToks you did this week. That side-by-side thing with Bear cooking and you flailing in front of a camp stove."

"Duet," I supply.

"Yeah. I wasn't sure it was exactly the message we'd want you to send about your skills, but Lucy convinced me. She says we take ourselves too seriously, sometimes, and we should let your spirit of fun shine through more."

"People loved that one," I say. It got tens of thousands of views and kicked off more views of several others.

Gabe opens his mouth to say something else, but just then the football players swarm back up onto the deck, sweaty and laughing and congratulating or roasting each other, as necessary. Hanna crosses to us and drifts close enough that I can feel the heat of her body. I want to reach out, wrap an arm around her, and draw her to my side.

Buck trots up the deck steps alongside his people.

"What's in his mouth?" Gabe demands. He reaches for his dog and pries his jaw open, removing—

"Nooooo," Hanna and I groan in unison.

Everyone turns to look at me. Then at Hanna. Then back at me. Then at the piece of fabric in Gabe's hand. It's a scrap of well-chewed purply fabric.

"Your sweatshirt," Gabe says to Hanna, just as Buck convulses, coughs, and heaves up a small pile of purple-fabric puke.

At my feet.

37

HANNA

Easton goes pale.

Heads swivel from Easton to me, and back again.

"Buck ate Hanna's sweatshirt!" Amanda's son Noah cries. "And barfed it on Easton's shoes! That means they have to get together! Auntie Hanna and Uncle Easton, up in a tree, K-I-S-S-I-N-G," Noah chants, and his younger brother, Kieran, joins in, with relish.

"Hush," Amanda says sharply. "Go. Heath—?!" She sends a pleading glance at her husband, who says, "Who wants to play Flyers Up?" and then descends the deck, followed by a Pied Piper wave of children.

Gabe stares at me. Then he turns to level his stony gaze at Easton.

"Now would be a good time to tell me if Lucy's right and I'm wrong and Buck's prognostication is bullshit," he growls.

I look at Easton. He looks at me. I bite my lip. I can tell the color of my face is approximately strawberry.

"I'm still waiting," Gabe says, crossing his arms.

When neither of us says anything, he throws up his hands in exasperation. "I guess that's my answer, then? Good to know. Would have been nicer if someone had told me." And then, "For fuck's sake, Easton, isn't *anything* sacred to you? She *works* for us. She's practically your sister."

Even under the very tense circumstances, I have to snort at that. And Easton's eyes snap to mine, alarm flashing over to amusement for a split second.

"Gabe, calm down," Lucy murmurs. She has appeared —thankfully, suddenly—at my side, garden hose in hand. "Don't make a fool of yourself. You're the only one of us who hasn't seen this coming like a train barreling down a track on the open plains."

"Him and me, both," Easton says quietly, and his eyes find mine again.

"I knew it!"

That's Brody.

"We *all* knew it."

That's Rachel, dryly.

Lucy takes that moment to turn the hose on the deck and Easton's shoes; he curses and jumps out of the way, then kicks off his (probably very nice, but I wouldn't know) loafers.

Gabe, still visibly wound up, starts in, "Jesus, E, I asked you to do *one* thing, not to draw attention away from Bear—"

But before he can go any further, Lucy grabs his arm. "Gabe," she says. "What did you think all the sparring was about? You of all people should know what it looks like when two people don't want to admit how they feel about each other."

Gabe looks from me to Easton and back again, a question on his face, but I can't answer. My stomach is tight. I know Lucy means well, but she's going too far, she's reading too much in, and I'm waiting for the other shoe to fall, for Easton to say, "Luce, don't make it more than it is. This isn't you and Gabe. This is just a summer fling, two people working off a little tension. I'm just helping Hanna with her sex drought."

Meanwhile they're all staring at us, wide-eyed, a murmur still moving among them, interest and speculation and delight.

The tightness in my stomach turns to churn.

And then rescue comes from a totally unexpected quarter. "Hey," Amanda says, suddenly at my side. "Han. Help me set up the make-your-own-sundae station?"

Gratefully, I follow her into the kitchen. I know the price of this rescue will be the third degree at her hands, but to my surprise, once we're in the kitchen, she only bustles around, handing me things and pointing me to where they need to be. She doesn't crow or giggle or welcome me to the family. She doesn't shoot me knowing glances.

She doesn't ask me anything.

Best of all, when all the sundae stuff is set out and I swallow the lump in my throat and say, "Thank you," she doesn't ask, "for what?"

EASTON WALKS me out to my truck.

"So, that wasn't so bad, right?"

After Buck blew our cover and Amanda magicked me off the porch and into the kitchen, no one mentioned Buck's sweatshirt shenanigans again. When she and I returned to the deck to announce that sundaes were ready, everyone dashed past me to their ice cream. No one gave me so much as a knowing look or a sly sideways glance. It was like it had never happened.

"It was weird," I say.

"Weird...?"

"Your family—I mean, aside from Gabe—was so—low-key about it. Since when do they just let something drop like that?"

"What?"

"You know how they are. All the teasing, all the wink-wink-nudge-nudge. So I was just wondering why. Why they made the kids pipe down and didn't give me the whole song and dance."

I was wondering, if I was being totally honest with myself, if maybe it was because they knew it had to be just a fling. If, like me, they knew Easton well enough to know that nothing more could ever come of it. Maybe they didn't make a big thing out of it because they didn't think it could *be* a big thing.

"Because they *love* you."

My mouth falls open.

"They know you hate being the center of attention, and they know you hate talking about your feelings. They dropped it so they wouldn't put you on the spot."

"They said that?"

"They didn't have to say it, Han. It's completely obvious. They love you so much, and they want to do whatever they need to do to show you. I know you don't always feel like you belong, but I'm telling you, you do. At least as much as any other Wilder."

"I'm not a Wilder."

"Of course you're a fucking Wilder," Easton says, sounding a little angry. "You just can't *see* it because people hurt you. Your dad. Your brothers. Your mom, even, by trying to make you fit some image of you she had, and then by—" He doesn't finish the sentence, but I know he means, *by dying.* "It wasn't her fault, but she hurt you." He draws me close. "I will kill the next person who tries, though."

I don't think I've ever heard Easton sound that serious. That certain. My chest feels tight. His strong arms are banded around me, and it feels like they're the only thing holding me together. Like if he lets go, I'll fly apart.

"Please," I beg.

I don't know what I'm asking for, but Easton does. He lowers his mouth to mine.

Instantly, the kiss catches fire, Easton groaning into my mouth, his hands roaming my body, pulling me tight against him. His strong thighs against mine, his cock hard between us, my hips reaching, rolling, craving more.

Voices penetrate our fog—the sound of more people calling out goodbyes as they leave the party—and Easton pulls back unwillingly, his fingertips on my face. His eyes tender.

"No one else is going to hurt you," he repeats.

Even you? I want to demand, because I'm starting to understand how big and impossible what I really want is.

I'm starting to understand that I've made it messy and complicated and that there's pain and disappointment on the other side.

And still, I don't think there's any way I'll be able to stop.

Amanda's whole family is tromping towards us, towards their car, calling out, "Bye Uncle Easton! Bye Hanna!!"

"Bye, you all! We love you!" Easton says.

When they're gone, we stand there, suddenly awkward.

"Uh, yeah. I should... go?" I say.

"I'm going to follow you home."

I open my mouth to protest, but Easton holds up a hand. "You don't have to invite me in. This isn't for that. It's just because I know you had a long night and I want to make sure you get home safe."

"You know I will."

"I want to see it with my own eyes."

His tone brooks no argument.

This Easton, this serious, sure man, is unfamiliar and yet someone I knew all along was inside him. I knew because of all those times he was in the right place, pressing a stone into my hand, standing beside me, making sure I had what I needed.

And what I needed was him. All those times.

I don't want him to just follow me home, give me a kiss outside our cars, and watch me walk up the porch steps.

I want so much more.

38

EASTON

I know her so well. I know her expression. There's something she wants that she won't let herself ask for.

"Tell me," I say. "Tell me what you want."

She shakes her head.

"You're going to make me guess."

She nods.

"You want to come home with me?"

She's never spent the night. On the Bear trip, she crawled out of my tent and back to hers. After the naked ice cream, I asked her to stay, but she said she'd promised her grandfather she'd make him a big breakfast in the morning before a fishing trip.

It's strange to spend so long not knowing what you want —not knowing, even, that you want *anything*—and then suddenly to have everything make perfect sense.

"We can leave your truck here."

Panic flashes in her eyes.

"They all know already, Han."

She nods. "Yeah. But."

"But what?"

I have never wanted her to trust me, trust this, more than right this second.

Her eyes flick to her truck. To my face. To my car. And then she nods, a small, tight *yes*.

I exhale. I hadn't even realized I was holding my breath. Waiting for her, like a verdict.

She gets into the car next to me. The now-familiar scent of her, a whole garden of exotic blooms, follows her. My mouth is dry, my chest tight. I'm nervous again, the way I was the first time we kissed. Like someone on the edge of a high board at the Olympics. Everything I've ever done before was practice for this because it never mattered until now.

I drive us back to my place, come around to open her door. She stands up, colliding with me. It's not some well-rehearsed move, not for either of us. It's guileless and grace-less, two bodies wanting to be as a close as possible as quickly as possible. "Hanna," I gasp because the feel of her against me is perfectly too much.

She tugs my hand, leading me toward my building, and I laugh, at how bossy and eager she is, and she looks back at me and laughs, too.

"I'm never going to be cute and meek," she says.

"Bullshit. You're cute. You're so fucking cute." I catch up to her, grab her head, and kiss her pink cheeks, making her blush deeper. "But good on not being meek. I've never had a thing for meek."

We race up the stairs together. I unlock my door and wrestle it open, and then we collapse against the inside of it, kissing. Our mouths are open and greedy, our tongues clashing and demanding. I fall to my knees, tug off her shoes, and wrestle her leggings down, smiling at the heather gray cotton thong she's wearing—even when she's impossibly sexy, she's so very, very Hanna.

"I like this," I say, running a finger down the center of the small triangle of fabric, making her shiver. I do it again, watching her. Her head falls back against the door, her eyes closing. I'm already so hard. I want to bury myself inside her… but not until she's ready for it. Way more than ready. I want her hungry and helplessly begging.

So, I spend a long time on my knees in front of her, tracing every edge of the thong, stroking her through the soft, practical cloth. Learning where the teasing feels best to her, what makes her tip her hips up for more, what makes her moan. I stroke down, too, to where the fabric narrows and I can feel her labia starting to swell with arousal, where her slickness makes the cloth and her body silky. I touch with fingers, with my tongue, with an open-mouthed kiss that makes her choke out my name. I tug the thong to the side so I can slide a finger inside her, and I nuzzle higher up, through the cloth, giving her heat and friction over her clit.

"Easton…"

"You want something?"

"More."

I smile against her mound. "Yeah?"

"Please."

"I like how you've accepted that your lot in life is going to be begging me for pleasure."

She groans. "You're Satan."

"Hardly. Would Satan do this?" I lick through the cloth, nipping and grinding until she's panting and trying to ride my face.

"Probably," she gasps.

I tug her panties down, lift one of her legs to my shoulder, and go to work in earnest, kissing and licking and circling.

"Easton."

"That's right, Han. Say it."

"Easton!"

I work her clit until she goes over the edge, shuddering and clutching my hair and crying my name.

She sags back against the door; I struggle to my feet, reaching for her.

"Legs around my waist," I order.

She obliges without protest, and I carry her to my bedroom, lowering her, limp and smiling dreamily, onto the edge of the bed.

I grin at her. "I like you like this. You're too blissed out to give me a hard time."

"Oh, I can still give you a hard time. Just give me a minute to recover."

"Nope," I say. I tug her shirt up, unfasten her bra, toss both to the floor. Then I strip out of my clothes.

"Just stand there and let me worship you," she says.

"Nope," I say again. "I'm in a hurry." I open the nightstand drawer and pull out a condom, rolling it on. Despite my words, I take a little extra time with it, because she's watching my every move, her pupils huge and dreamy. I wouldn't want to deprive her of her fun.

Who am I kidding? I love her eyes on me.

I give her a little push, and she falls backwards onto the bed, laughing. I crawl up between her legs. "Mmm," I say, fingers parting her so I can slide my cock through her folds —not into her core, not yet. Just following the same exploratory paths that my fingers did earlier—all those sensitive curves and folds, and the hard bud of her clit, now so sensitive that she gasps when the head of my cock finds her and I stroke her, back and forth.

"Too much?"

"God. No."

I work myself against her until her eyes close and her mouth opens; then I line my cock up and very gently nudge inside.

The deep gasp-groan she lets out is extremely gratifying.

"You like that?"

"So much."

"Is it helping with the 'it's been a while' problem?"

"Mmm. Not sure yet. Keep going? I'll let you know."

I chuckle. Of course sex with Hanna is like this— combative, playful, fun. All that foreplay I didn't know I was having. All those times our back-and-forth turned me on, and I couldn't admit to myself how very, very much I wanted to tussle with her in a completely different way.

Now I can. And it's—

Well, it's hard to hold back, but it's been a long time for her, and I don't want to hurt her, not even a little. So, I only take what she gives. I push in just a fraction at a time, stealing more depth in her core as her cheeks pink up and her lips redden and her eyelashes cast shadows on her skin, her eyes drifting closed in pleasure. And I'm not complaining. She's so, so tight. Snug around my cock, hot and wet and perfect.

I slide a hand down between us and idly play, enjoying the whimpers I can pull out of her. She yields more to me, and I take it, making her moan.

I could do this all night.

Until she clenches her inner muscles around my cock.

"Are you doing that on purpose?"

"Mmm-hmm."

She's strong.

"Unngh. Hanna, stop. You're going to make me come if you keep doing that."

"I don't want to stop. It feels too good."

It does. It feels so fucking good.

I press my thumb to her clit and circle it. She throws her head back against the pillow, lifts her hips, and whimpers, her grip on me suddenly erratic and pulsing.

"Are you *coming*?" I demand. "God, that's hot. That's so fucking hot."

I thrust into her, and she cries out, clutching my ass, raking her fingernails down my back, biting into my shoulder. "More," she says.

I oblige, not holding anything back, plunging deep inside her, filling her, getting my fill of her.

She's softened and gone boneless under me again, but that's okay because she's gazing up at me with big blue trusting eyes. And I've never been much for eye-contact during sex—it always feels like too much—but I can't look away from her. This woman, this friend, this funny, smart, very hot person who makes me feel more like myself than

I've ever felt in my life, who already fits my world like she was made for it, and all I want is this. Her.

My chest is bursting with emotion, my throat, my eyes —it's like there's nowhere for it all to go, and it's coiling inside me, rising in a spiral up my spine, boiling from my root, and I'm clutching her like a drowning man, coming so hard it's all I can do to hold on, calling her name over and over.

39

HANNA

I wake up with a hundred and ninety pounds of extremely well-crafted man wrapped around me. His beautiful, sculpted arm drapes over me, his calloused outdoorsy-guy hand rests on my breast. His nose is tucked in my hair, his erection pressing into my lower back.

"Hey," he murmurs.

"Hey, yourself."

He tugs me closer. "I have an idea," he says. "We shower…"

"Separately?"

"Fuck no," he says, grinding on me.

I giggle.

"And then we go get breakfast pastries at Rush Creek bakery."

I try to picture it. Nan, Rush Creek's resident gossip, owns the Rush Creek bakery, and there will be no end of *talk* if the two of us show up together for breakfast. On the other hand, as Easton pointed out last night, everyone who matters already knows.

"Okay," I say.

"Yeah?" he asks, like he hadn't been expecting me to say yes.

"Yeah."

I can't decide which I love more, soaping up the hard planes of Easton's body or the moment when he takes the soap from me and returns the favor, his fingers knowing and skillful. He crowds me from behind, takes my hands, and lifts them to the cool tile, gliding his thick erection over my soapy skin.

"Here," I say, lifting down the detachable shower head. "Get that soap off."

He does. He reaches for the condom he's balanced on the shower's shelf, and in a feat of athleticism that's probably par for the course for men named Wilder, pins me against the wall and—with shower head in one hand and himself in the other—enters me from behind.

He's hard and thick and fills me completely, and when he turns the detachable nozzle on my clit, his long, callused fingers holding me open to his ministrations, I'm helpless. I come, weak-kneed, clawing the tile.

"Oh, fuck, Han, you feel so good—"

His words fall apart to groans, grunts, shouts, his body rigid behind me.

"I didn't realize how handy this thing was," he says, looking down at the shower head he's holding. He's still inside me, and I'm still throbbing around him.

"Men never do," I say. "Now you know."

"I have *lots* of ideas about how to use this knowledge," he says, slowly releasing me. He hangs the shower head and reaches for towels just outside the steamy glass door. Hands me one.

"E," I say, caressing the thick plush. "I don't think I've ever used a towel this nice."

He shrugs. "I like nice things."

"Maybe that should be your new Wilder identity. The Nice Things brother."

"Ha," he says.

"The Good With Oral brother?"

He grins. "You really think they'd let me take that one for myself?"

"No. Definitely not."

He takes the towel from me and rubs me down gently. It feels amazing. I think I purr.

"You know what I think?" I say, when I pop my head back out of the fluffiness. "I think you're the Just the All Around Best Wilder."

I say it in the same spirit of teasing that I made my other suggestions, but his eyes, when I meet them, are serious. Tender and, I think, a little wistful. "Yeah?" he says.

"Yeah."

My own chest hurts, and I need to say something to deflect. "But don't let it go to your head."

He smiles at that, and the softness in his expression fades. The moment feels like a delicate bubble I've popped. And I want to bring it back... but I don't know how. I search for the right words, the true words, the soft words, but I don't know what they are or how to put them together. How to express what Easton is to me: as welcome as the right rock pressed into my palm, as substantial and comforting as the weight of a worry stone in my pocket, as playful as one skipping across the surface of the river.

But somehow, "you're the skipping stone brother," doesn't seem like it'll sound as good spoken out loud as it does in my head.

Easton takes longer than I do to get ready, which doesn't surprise either of us. I sit cross-legged on the bed and realize it's been several days since I checked my emails.

There are emails from four of my brothers, four of five replies to my "party for granddad" subject line, and my heart squeezes, a strange heavy thud.

I read all four emails, then slump back against the pillows on Easton's bed.

Four nos.

My brothers are polite but firm. As human beings, they couldn't be more different from each other, but their answers all follow a formula: *too busy, but even if I weren't, I can't imagine coming back there to celebrate that pain in my ass. But please, come visit! I've got plenty of space, and I miss you.*

And I can't blame them for not wanting to come back. They all lost a lot, too, and unlike me, none of them could see the squishy heart beating under my granddad's rough exterior... but...

"Hey," Easton says quietly. "You okay?"

"Yeah," I lie.

He squints at me. "Han."

"I'm fine."

He sighs. "Let me try another tack. What did you just see on your phone?"

Even in the face of a direct question, my brain squirms, trying to find a way around admitting how unsettled I am, but in the end, I give in.

"My brothers aren't coming to my granddad's party. Well, four of them aren't coming. My email to Tuck straight-up bounced."

Which means he changed his email address and didn't tell me.

That one hurts. A lot.

Honestly, they all hurt.

Easton sits down on the bed next to me.

"See?" I challenge him, intending to tease. "You can't keep me from getting hurt."

But the words don't come out teasing. They come out bitter and raw.

He winces. "No," he says, "I guess I can't. But I wish I could. Hanna, you don't know how much I wish I could."

There's a long silence. I want to tell him I do know, and that he's always been the best bulwark against hurt, but it feels so big and serious, and I'm too scraped up inside to risk it. He's quiet, too, his shoulders a little hunched.

I hate this, the awkwardness that always comes with soul baring, and I don't know how to get back to where we were, back to the teasing and the tenderness.

"Hey," I say. "Sorry to bail on the breakfast plans, but I'm feeling like maybe I'd rather just... I don't know, go home and sulk?"

"Of course," he says, a little stiffly. "I'll take you back to your truck, how 'bout?"

"Perfect," I say. It's not perfect, not at all. There's nothing perfect about the way I feel right now, suddenly brittle, but I don't know how to talk about it.

His gaze scrapes over my face, searching, and I want him to find what he's looking for, but I can't stand how exposed I feel, so I look away.

We head outside together, pile into his Jeep, and drive back to Wilder headquarters to retrieve my truck.

But when we get there, Bear is just stepping out of *his* truck in the parking lot. He looks from Easton to me and back again.

"Hey," Bear says. "We... okay?"

He looks from me to Easton and back to me.

I nod. Easton takes a moment longer, but then he does, too, his expression softening.

Bear holds out a slip of paper. "I'm sorry this took me so long, E, but I've got a job offer for you." He presses the offer into my hands. "Salary's on there. Think you're gonna like it."

Easton unfolds the paper, and I can tell just by looking at his face that whatever it says on that paper, it's way more than he ever thought he'd make.

"Basically, you'll get to write your own job description, too. Consider that my apology for fucking up with the video. And consider it my promise that nothing like that will happen again on my watch."

Easton's mouth is open; he clearly wasn't expecting that, or the promise of so much freedom in the new job. And my insides feel like they're made of wet cement.

I knew this was coming. I knew being with Easton was a time-bound thing. I knew I'd lose him. And it's better, so much better, to lose him to Bear and Colorado and something he loves doing than to... well, whatever's going to happen next. To him getting bored or moving on to someone else.

That thought makes me sick to my stomach; I can't believe how many times I joked about him melting a pair of panties that didn't belong to me.

I will never, ever be able to joke about Easton Wilder's sex life again. Not as long as I live.

40

EASTON

I'm still feeling like I got run over by a semi-trailer when Bear tells me, again, to "think about it" and heads inside.

I clutch the paper with Bear's obscene salary proposal in one hand. More money than I let myself want... and a "write your own job description" offer.

"You look like you're going to throw up," Hanna observes. "Is that happy barfing?" She doesn't wait for me to answer. "You should be happy. A super famous celebrity wants to pay you ridiculous money to do exactly what you want to do. It's your dream come true!"

It's true that it's what I thought I wanted. To get out of Rush Creek, away from what felt like stifling sameness and being perennially under my big brother's thumb. To be taken seriously enough to get paid what I'm worth and given the work I'm excited about.

But right now? It doesn't feel like what I want at all.

Rush Creek hasn't felt stifling these last few weeks. It's felt like...

It's felt like what I didn't let myself know I wanted. Discovering that the woman who makes me laugh is also the woman who gets me hotter than I've ever been, who gets me off... but most of all? Who *gets* me.

Hanna, who doesn't let anyone in, has let me in in so many different ways, and I've never felt connected to another person the way I feel connected to her.

These last few weeks in Rush Creek? They've felt like possibility and the future, like the beginning of the rest of my life.

I open my mouth to say that. To say that everything's changed for me, that what I thought I wanted doesn't matter anymore, because the thing I want now wins out over everything else. But Hanna is already speaking, her tone teasing.

"It's kind of the perfect ending," she says. "You get the job of your dreams, you move away. Better that it ends like this, right? Before it has a chance to end in disaster."

"Don't *do* that," I say, irritably. "Why do you do that? Talk like there's no way it could possibly work?"

I know I'm hurt and frustrated because I'm thinking about beginnings and she's talking about endings, but I can't seem to be cool about it.

"Because there's no way it could possibly work," she says. "You just got offered a job in Colorado."

And then she shrugs, like it's nothing. Like my going to Colorado, like things between us ending, is nothing to her.

I frown. "I don't have to take it."

"You *should* take it. You want it. Obviously, you do, or you would have told Bear you didn't want the job. But you didn't tell him that, did you? You do *want* it."

And she's right. I want it. I want to do what I love and be taken seriously. I want to make my own way, not just the Wilder way.

I just...

...want something else, more.

I say, "I want this." I repeat it, point to the two of us, so there's no mistake. "I want this, you and me."

"You want—"

She's staring at me like I've said something so absurd, she can't even assimilate it.

"Like a relationship," she says. "You want us to be —together?"

"Don't you?"

"I don't... I don't know," she says. "What would that mean? You'd turn down the Bear job and stay here? When you know you're sick of working for your brother and not being taken seriously? How long do you think that would work for you before you realized you'd made a mistake?"

"You could come to Colorado," I say. "Bear knows a ton of people doing outdoors stuff in the Golden area. For that matter, so do I. We could have you hooked up in a second."

She frowns and looks away. "You know I can't do that, E. I've got my granddad here—he's all I've got left, and the day is coming soon when he won't be able to manage all the ranch admin himself. And, well, I love working for Wilder. On its worst day, it's my dream job."

I know that's all true, and I don't begrudge her one ounce of it, but a vise tightens in my gut.

Some part of me must have been expecting this to go down very differently. Some part of me must have thought that when I told her how I felt, that I wanted us to stay together, she'd throw her arms around me and squeal with delight. In all the years I was sleeping around, I'd never really thought about what *not* wanting to be done with someone would feel like. What it would feel like to ask for more and not get it.

The universe doles out hard lessons, and I can see from the look on Hanna's face that this one's not done yet.

"You've *never* had a girlfriend, E," she says. "You've never been serious about anyone. And I'm… I don't want… I can't be your practice girlfriend."

The anger that had been heating up in me grinds to a cold, slow stop.

"You don't… you really don't think we can make this work."

It's not a question. Because I know I'm right.

"We didn't set out to make this work, E," she says quietly. "We knew who we both were." Her eyes scan my face, looking, I think, for confirmation that I know I'm asking for something absurd, that I know I've gone way off script.

She's right, of course. We didn't set out for this to be *something*.

It was always temporary in her mind.

We both knew who we both were.

I'm temporary.

Which makes sense because I've always been temporary. I'm the one-night guy, the just-for-fun guy. The jokester.

The flirt.

I'm good at *temporary*, and I shouldn't be surprised that

I got chosen for *temporary* by someone who has seen me excel at it my whole life.

Hanna doesn't think we can make this work. But worse, she never *has*.

"I just think—you should take the job. It's a sure thing, Easton. A sure way for you to be happy. And I think it's the universe's way of putting a clean ending on what's between us." She says it decisively, like a lawyer making a closing statement.

"What if I don't want a clean ending?" I ask. "What if I want—"

Caution is screaming inside my head. *Don't do it! This is Hanna, and you know her, you can't just come at her with all the words and all the feelings. You're going to scare her, and that's going to make it worse.*

But I'm hurt and frustrated. I want her to be in it with me, to take me seriously, to believe that we are—that I am—enough to make this work.

"What if I want it all? The future. Forever. Marriage. Children. Happily ever after? What if I want that, Hanna?"

Hanna's eyes get big, and her face fills with something. If I trusted myself, I'd say it was *hope*. And I feel it too. I've finally said the right thing; I've finally convinced her I'm serious; I've finally gotten through.

And then that bright emotion in her eyes vanishes. She takes a step backward, a small stumble. Just a half-step hitch.

"You don't," she says, shaking her head. Her eyes are big. Panicked. "You don't want that. You think you do, but you'll get bored of me. You'll get tired of this. You'll want the job you turned down when the sex was shiny and new.

And when you do, I'll be the one who loses everything. You. Your family. My friends. My job. That's how it works."

She's shaking her head.

"Hanna."

"Don't," she says. So familiar. *Don't give me that stone, don't give me that kiss, don't give me that compliment.*

Only this time, it's *don't need me*, and there's nothing I can do about it, because it's way, way too late.

41

HANNA

After I say, *Don't*, Easton stops talking. He keeps looking at me with the same lost, puzzled expression, but he doesn't try to talk me into anything anymore.

"I should go," I say, and turn away from him, heading for my truck.

I half expect him to call me back, but he doesn't, and I'm glad. As I start the engine, I'm nothing but relieved.

Holding onto that thought, trying my best not to think about shared showers or skipped stones or anything of the things that might wreck me, I steer the truck toward the ranch.

So. I did it. It's over. And the world didn't end. I'm still… standing. My stomach feels jostled, like I've just stepped off a boat at the end of a long stormy ride, but I'm intact.

Easton will go to Colorado, I'll stay here, and I'll tuck all the loose ends in, like yarn strands into an aging sweater. I'll tell my friends the truth, that it was just a fling, a brief loss of sanity, a sex snack. I'll go back to trying to find a guy who's not too famous, not too married, and not too weird, or I'll just... take a break.

If my mother had been able to tell a fling from a serious relationship, she might not have let her movie-star boyfriend get her pregnant when she landed in LA as a naive striver.

Or twice more after he'd grudgingly married her.

And if she hadn't leapt into—and been smacked out of —that first marriage, she might not have fallen so quickly into a second one—and the two kids that rapidly followed.

And for sure, after that marriage ended, if good sense had prevailed, she never would have let herself fall for my father, a barrel racer who, from the very beginning, told her that she could never compete with the rodeo.

She should have known better, just like I should have known better.

I park the truck and head inside.

"Hanna, that you?" my grandfather calls out.

"Yup!" I call back, coming into the living room. "Got a bunch of work to do! I'll be in my room!"

"You hear anything from those brothers of yours?"

"Nope!" I lie. I keep my voice light and cheerful, and I almost believe myself.

My grandfather's grumbling follows me down the hall.

I step into my bedroom. It's still the same bedroom, the bedroom I didn't let my mom decorate in pink. I sink down onto the bed and grab Leonard the pink bear, wrap my arms around him.

This is good, I think. This is neat and tidy. Not messy, like we feared. Not complicated. It's its own kind of happily ever after, in which Easton and I each go on to do what's right for us, him in Colorado, me in Rush Creek. When he comes home to visit, we'll give each other crap in the old way, and this summer will be just a strange detour from a long-standing frenemyship.

But as my hand touches the hem of my tank top to pull it over my head—I've been in these clothes two days now—I pause. Stroke my fingers over the soft material of the first outfit Easton helped me pick out. I can still see him standing to my side and just behind, his reflection in the mirror as his eyes traveled over my body.

Being wanted isn't a small thing.

There are lots of people in the world, and most of them see only whatever part of you they need to see.

But for a short time, it felt like Easton saw all of me. And that the more he saw, the more he wanted to see, until there wasn't anything else left to hide from him...

Except how much I wanted him to keep wanting to see and know more.

As I peel my clothes off, it's like I'm peeling him off. Peeling away our time together, this magic summer, all the kisses and touches, the small gifts—stones and t-shirts and boy shorts and his presence.

When I'm naked, I put on my comfiest, baggiest, rattiest old clothes, hoping they'll remind me that I'm still me, no matter what gets peeled away.

I settle myself against my pillow, open the Netflix app and find *Bridgerton*, Season One.

I start watching again, from the beginning.

After a while, I reach out and pull Leonard the pink bear into my arms, because he's better than nothing.

But I don't cry.

42

EASTON

As I carefully sand a panel of the kayak I'm building, I hear Brody's voice behind me.

"Thought I might find you here."

I'm in the big storage shed behind Wilder Headquarters, half of which has been semi-permanently granted to me for boat work.

"Texted you a bunch of times and didn't get an answer," Brody says. He's keeping it casual. "You didn't show up for guys' night out."

"Wasn't in the mood," I say.

"Hanna didn't show up either." His voice is careful.

"She doesn't always."

"True," Brody says. "But you do."

I don't look at him.

"E," he says. "You know we're all talking about you, right? And the longer you hide from us, the more people are speculating and making shit up. We're Wilders. If you hide out here for too long, we're going to write you a whole

Titanic-level drama. Everyone wants to know what the fuck's going on with you and Hanna."

"Nothing's going on."

"Right," Brody says, with a short, harsh laugh. "That's why neither of you denied that Buck has supernatural powers after he barfed on Easton's feet."

I close my eyes. I haven't seen Hanna for more than a week. Or to be more exact, we haven't spoken. I've seen her all right—leaving headquarters shortly after I arrive, spending time with her girlfriends instead of the guys, eating her lunch alone to avoid me. And still, my strongest impulse is to tease her—

What, you avoiding me? Afraid you'll be so overwhelmed by my hotness you won't be able to resist?

But of course, I don't. We've finally done the thing she was afraid of: We've finally broken the friendship. There's no going back, apparently.

"Nothing *is* going on? Or nothing *was* going on?"

I should have known that Brody, of all my brothers, would see clear to the bottom of my bullshit. "Nothing *is*." I sigh.

"You want to tell me about it?" he asks.

"Not really."

"Let me rephrase," he says. "Do you want to tell me about it here, while you keep working on the boat? Or do you want to come to Oscar's with me and do a few shots and then tell me about it?"

"Why don't you ever let a man sulk in peace?" I demand.

"Because I'm your brother," Brody says. "That's what having four brothers is all about. You can't spend the time you want on the toilet, you can't have secrets, and you can't sulk by yourself."

Against my will, I smile. "I'm afraid if I start drinking, I won't stop."

"Fair enough," he says. He tips over an oversized bucket that at one point held varnish but is now bone dry, and sits on it, planting his hands on his thighs.

"Start talking."

IT TAKES LONGER than I expect to bring him up to date… probably because when I open my mouth to tell the short story, a novel comes pouring out. I tell him about how Hanna went on her date with Bear. How the world thought they were the cutest couple ever. How Hanna said the kiss with Bear was *fine*.

And I tell him what happened next. The PG version.

But the X-rated version is very much alive in my mind.

Just remembering it makes my chest hot and my throat tight with recalled desire and current misery.

Brody listens quietly and watches my face like it's playoff football. Of course it has to be Brody who's in charge of giving me the third degree—the one brother I can't bullshit.

I tell him how one thing led to another, a tumble of desire and getting-to-know-you that, to me, felt more and more right and inevitable.

He nods. Like he knows. Like he's been there. I know he has because I know the story of how he and Rachel met. Two opposites who weren't supposed to be together, unable to resist the pull of circumstance and chemistry. Sex toys on a boat and grappling in Brody's truck, and lots and lots of *feelings*.

I lead him right up through the gathering when Buck did his messy magic trick.

"She went home with me that night," I say.

He shrugs. "Yeah, so I heard. Left her truck at Gabe's. No one was surprised by then."

Even though I don't want to, I can see her, the vivid pinks and reds of her face, her eyes closing in pleasure.

"It was—" I shake my head. Laugh, without much humor.

Brody laughs, too. "Been there, buddy. It's a whole different ball game when you care, right?"

"Scary different," I admit.

He nods in quiet solidarity.

"Except... The next morning... I thought we were on the same page. I didn't think we had to put words to it. I thought we understood each other."

"There's your first mistake," Brody says. Not mean. Just matter of fact. "You can't know what's in someone's head unless you ask."

"Well. I thought I knew."

I open my mouth to talk about what happened next, and I realize: It won't make sense unless I tell him everything.

He's waiting. Patient.

The truth's going to come out at some point. Might as well get a preview of how my family's going to react when they find out I've been flirting with a competitor.

"Bear offered me a job in Colorado," I say. It's skipping

over a lot of backstory, but I think it gets across most of what he needs to know.

"Whaaaaa—?" It's more a noisy huff of disbelief than a word. His eyes search my face, and he sees the truth there. "And you're seriously thinking about taking it."

"I was. And then I wasn't. And now I am."

"And Hanna got pissed? That you were leaving?"

"I wish." My chest hurts. "No. She told me to take it."

"Did you tell her you didn't want it? Did you tell her you wanted her?"

I sigh. "Yeah. I told her I wanted it all. Future, marriage, babies. And she said…" I feel slightly unhinged, but I crush it down, ruthlessly. "She said 'Don't.' Like, stop talking like that, Easton. Like, I don't want to hear it."

Brody winces.

"Yeah," I say.

"Do you think maybe she—?"

I'm already shaking my head as he finishes, "—misunderstood? Didn't know how you felt?"

"No. I was pretty dang clear."

"Are you sure—?"

"Hey," I say, as gently as I can, when I hurt all over like I've been bruised in a fight. "Yeah. I'm sure."

Brody dips his head. "I'm sorry, E."

"Not half as sorry as I am."

We're both quiet for a minute, while I try not to think about how much I already miss her—being together, touching, laughing. How if I could, I'd go back to how it was before, just to know we could still joke around. Just to know that if she needed me, I could still find her and tuck a stone into the palm of her hand and stand by, quietly.

Brody's voice cuts through my thoughts. "So—tell me about the job."

I do, starting with the day Bear came to town and I asked him if the job was available, ending with the offer in the parking lot.

When I'm done, he says, "Does Gabe know?"

I shake my head.

"You gonna tell him?"

"Yes, of course. I'm not just going to leave town and let him figure it out."

"Any chance you'd let him make a counteroffer?"

I burst out laughing. "A *what*?"

But Brody's apparently not joking. "A counteroffer. You tell him what Bear's giving you, and he matches it."

"No way he could match this kind of money."

"And that's what it's about? The money?"

"No."

"Then...?"

I don't answer right away, and Brody watches me quietly. "Can I tell you something?" he says, finally, when I still haven't spoken.

"Shoot."

"It took me a long time to tell Gabe what I needed from him. Because I didn't think I deserved it."

"It's not that," I say. "If that was how I felt, I wouldn't have asked Bear for a job, right? I know what I'm worth."

"I'm just saying, there are two kinds of Wilder brothers."

I raise an eyebrow. "Those that have 'married' sex, and me?"

Brody snorts. "Well, that too. But that's not what I was going to say. I was going to say, there are the ones who've known exactly what they're meant to be doing from the moment they were born, and the rest of us."

I think about my brothers, and it's obvious what he means. Gabe and Clark were made to be outdoorsmen, from minute one. But the rest of us—I know it's been more complicated for us. Brody was a rebel in high school and for years afterwards, a regular tear-it-up bad boy who hated rules and bucked Gabe's authority at every turn. Kane never quite seemed quite at ease with outdoor adventuring —and these days, he's doing a lot more photography and running photography trips.

And then there's me.

"Takes some of us a little longer to figure ourselves out," he says.

I bristle—it's not that I haven't figured myself out...

But then I think, have I?

I hadn't known how I felt about Hanna. I hadn't known how empty my flavor-of-the-week ice cream sex had gotten. And I hadn't known how much I wanted to be taken seriously until an outside opportunity came along and I jumped on it like a drowning man on a flimsy bit of a life raft.

Maybe that's a bad analogy.

But the point stands.

"So, what do I *do*?" I ask.

Brody smiles. "Fuck if I know," he says. "But the general shape is, figure out what you want, ask for it, and then hold on and don't let it go."

It takes me three more days to get up the courage to talk to Gabe. I knock on his office door early in the morning at work. It feels an awful lot like bearding a lion in its den.

"Hey," I say.

He squints at me, already suspicious.

"There's something I have to tell you."

"Yeah. I could tell. You have the same look on your face you used to get when you pulled a prank on one of us—and Mom caught you."

I wince. "Yeah. In this situation? You're sort of Mom."

"I figured. Spit it out, E."

"Bear Warden offered me a job."

His face goes white behind the omnipresent not-quite-a-beard scruff that Lucy must love.

"He offered you a job. Out of the blue?"

Gabe is many things. But not dumb.

"I may or may not have thrown my hat in a ring I knew was open."

His jaw tightens, and his eyes flash anger. "And when was this exactly?"

"When Bear showed up," I admit.

In theory, I could have lied. Made this a little less miserable for myself... but I'm a Wilder. We're straight up, once we know what it is we mean to say.

"You've known for, what, weeks? months? that you weren't happy with your job and you didn't think that was worth a mention to your boss and *brother*?"

"In fairness," I say, "people do that all the time. Try to get another job before they tell their bosses they're leaving."

"Their bosses, maybe, but their *brothers*?"

Brody had warned me that Gabe was going to play the brother card, hard. But I shake my head. "You know you can't be both in this case."

His eyes narrow, but he doesn't dispute that. "You've been applying for a job under my nose this whole summer."

"Yes."

He gets up and stalks away from me, planting a hand flat on the back wall of the office.

"You should have told me," he growls, facing me once more.

I'm surprised to discover that I'm calm. Maybe it's the sense that there's nothing to lose here, that I've already screwed up the only thing that really matters to me. But more likely it's that I've had a lot of time to think about what Brody said: *Figure out what you want, ask for it, and then hold on and don't let go.*

Pretty good life advice, no matter what arena you're in.

"I did what I thought I needed to do for my career."

His eyebrows go up.

"But I'm telling you now."

Because maybe it's too late… and maybe it's not.

"I can do a lot more than I'm doing, and I can do it a lot better if you give me more freedom. I can do for Wilder what Bear does for his own business. I can make us influencers online, and I can use that to bring in lots of advertising and also lots of new customers for the business. I just need you to let me do it. Oh, and I need you to let me hire an assistant."

His mouth is open now.

"Do you know why I wanted to work for Bear?" I ask. Because what I realized while talking to Brody yesterday was that sometimes I think I've asked for what I want, spoken out loud what's in my head, only to realize I'm thinking it so fucking loudly that it *feels* like the whole world should know.

He shakes his head.

"Because he doesn't see me as the comic relief. The littlest Wilder."

His expression morphs slowly. From surprise to something else. Something I don't recognize at first… but then slowly I do. Not apology. *Sympathy.*

"I didn't know," he says quietly. "I didn't know you hated what you were doing or that you wanted more or that the thing you wanted was to be an influencer. I didn't know that you didn't feel taken seriously or—I didn't know any of that. Because you didn't tell me."

And that's when I see it. That's when I finally get it.

"Oh," I say. "This was never about how you see me."

To his credit, Gabe stays quiet.

"It's about... how... I see me."

Still quiet. And I have to say, I have never loved my oldest brother as much as I do right this second. For all his faults, he knows how to shut the fuck up when it matters.

"I wasn't taking myself or what I wanted seriously."

He doesn't so much as shake or nod his head. He holds very still. Just letting me have my... moment. Or whatever it is. I feel like he'd let me talk to myself all day if that was what it took.

But honestly, I think I'm done. I get it now.

They were never going to take me seriously until I did. Not because they were mean or thoughtless, but because they couldn't see who I was and what I wanted and needed —until *I could.*

When he finally speaks, he says, "You have a year."

"What?"

"You have a year to make the influencer thing work for us. You can do it in a year, right? I can't hire someone to take over the water trips, so you'll still have to do that, but I'll do what you asked. I'll hire you an entry-level person to take over the admin duties for the water trips plus whatever you can give them for social media work. Will that do it?"

He asks the last grumpily, but I can see the warmth in his usually steely eyes. The affection.

"Are you giving me that because you're my boss? Or my brother?" I can't help asking.

He rolls his eyes. "I'm giving you what you asked for because I think it's going to make us *money*," he says.

That probably would have ended the discussion decisively, but I don't get a chance to find out for sure, because just then Brody knocks.

"Hey," he says, ducking his head in. "Everyone okay in here?"

"We're fine," Gabe says, waving a hand dismissively.

I'm glad he didn't think either of us was ever in danger of dying.

"I'm staying in Rush Creek," I tell Brody.

"Well, that's fantastic news," he says. "But I'm not actually surprised."

"I bet Hanna will be happy to hear it," Gabe says, eyebrows raised. "I imagine that's a big part of why you want to stay?"

Brody winces. I flinch.

"We broke up," I tell Gabe.

"You—broke *up* with her?" He roars his outrage. I try not to visibly cower.

"Actually," I say, "she broke up with me."

He covers his face with a big hand and rubs it up and down. "I don't understand. Lucy just finished telling me how you and Hanna were going to live happily ever after, even though I would have put my money on her offing you and burying the body. But no, Lucy says that, despite all the evidence to the contrary, you and Hanna are actually perfect for each other."

I scowl. "I hate that phrase, perfect for each other. People aren't *perfect* for each other. They're messy and rough-edged, they make things more complicated for each other. Hanna and I are..." I take a deep breath. "We're best friends. Or we were. I thought maybe we were soul mates. And then when it turned out that we—"

I get a brief flash of the way it was, Hanna and me in bed together, laughing, tumbling, clutching. So fucking good, head, heart, and body. "We weren't perfect for each other, but we were definitely *good* for each other."

Brody and Gabe are both staring at me.

"You're in love with her," Gabe says.

My mouth falls open. "I—"

But he's right. I mean, obviously he's right. That's what it means to want to spend all your time with someone, to want to be as physically close to them as you possibly can, to feel perfectly content when you're with them. In them.

For the first time since Hanna walked away, I let myself remember that perfect contentment.

Gabe's eyes scour my face. "And you *let her walk away*."

"Because she doesn't want what I want."

"And what you want is…?"

"Marriage. Babies. The whole shebang."

Gabe's eyebrows go into his hairline.

"Did you *tell* her that?"

"Gabe," Brody warns.

"Yeah, I told her," I say, wearily. My body aches. Maybe it's just my heart, but it feels an awful lot like the flu.

"Do you think she believed you?"

"I mean, yeah?"

My brothers look at each other. Then it's Brody's turn.

"He's got a point, E. I believe you. Gabe believes you. Because we know who you are and that you're not about saying shit you don't mean. But Hanna? It's new, right? New to us, new to her. All we knew of you until recently was the Easton you let us see. The one who wanted a different ice cream flavor every day of the week. The one who said just a couple of weeks ago maybe he wasn't the kind of guy who has a right person."

"But isn't that the whole point?" I demand. "I did! I found the right person, and everything changed."

"You know that. And I know that. But Hanna? Did you tell her that? Did you tell her, 'You're my right person.'"

I think about this. Hard. "I thought I did."

Gabe frowns. "But what exactly did you *say*, Easton? Did you tell her that you were in love with her? That you loved her?"

Gabe looks at me. Brody looks at me. I open my mouth. Close it again.

"No," I say.

I didn't, because somehow, I'd thought it was implicit in all the other things I was saying. Somehow, I'd thought it would be... obvious.

But would it? To Hanna?

A dad who left, a mom who died, a grandfather with limited emotional range and communication skills and brothers who, for their own reasons, needed to get the hell out of Rush Creek.

Leaving her...

Not trusting much.

Certainly not trusting that any man's motives—especially a man who'd spent most of his life, erm, sampling ice cream flavors—would be pure and, more to the point, *permanent*.

"Well," Brody says. "That might be your problem, right there."

I run my mind back over Hanna's and my last conversation.

I want *this*, I'd said. *You and me. The future. Forever. Marriage. Children.*

I'd asked her for a lot of things I didn't even know if she wanted—without giving her a chance to tell me if she did.

Without telling her *why* I wanted all those things with her... or more to the point, what I *really* wanted from her, which was just to be allowed to love her today and tomorrow, and if it worked for her, the day after that and the day after that, ad infinitum. The rest of it was really just details. I could take it or leave it.

"Shit," I say.

Brody smiles at that. "Been there, buddy," he says. "Gabe has too, but he might not be willing to admit it, because it will spoil his image as totally and completely in control of everything all the time."

Gabe rolls his eyes. "I've been there, too," he says grudgingly. "And Lucy isn't willing to let me pretend to be completely in control all the time anymore."

"Which is why the business is actually profitable now." Brody smirks.

"No thanks to you, boat boy..."

I slap a hand on Gabe's desk. "Guys! Quit it! Focus! What do I do now?"

They both gape at me.

Brody opens his mouth to say something, but before he can get the words out, I realize he's already told me what I need to know.

"Nope, never mind. I know the answer."

They both stare at me as I stand up and head for the door.

Over my shoulder, I call:

"Figure out what I want, ask for it, and then hold on and don't let it go."

44

———

EASTON

I pound on the front door of the ranch house.

"Easton Wilder, get the hell away from my front door," a voice rings out. It's Hanna's grandfather, and he's pissed.

"I've got a shotgun, and I've been waiting for a chance to use it on one of Hanna's deadbeats. You'd look great as a piece of Swiss cheese."

His voice is muffled by the door. Chances are, that gun —if it exists at all—is loaded with either rock salt or bird shot. Still, if he fires, he'll bust up the door and probably cut himself, and the last thing I want is to compound my sins with Hanna by hurting her granddad. And damaging the front door.

But.

I'm also not leaving without talking to Hanna.

"Is Hanna in there?"

"Pretty sure I made my position on that crystal clear," he bellows. "You stay the fuck away from her. She didn't come out of her room for three days, and when she did, her eyes were so red it looked like she'd been into the Willis-ton's weed harvest. Had to pry out of her what happened. I knew it had to be either you or the other asshole. Bear Nekkid or whatever his name is."

Bear Nekkid. As dire as the situation feels on all fronts right now, I have to smile.

"Mr. Hott? Any chance I could get you to open the door? And not shoot me? I have something to say to Hanna."

"Not a chance in this world."

"What if I said I love your granddaughter?"

There's a long silence. Then he says, "Don't ask me what if. You either love her or you don't."

"I love Hanna."

The door slowly swings open. "You have a shitty way of showing it." He lowers his Winchester and glowers at me.

"In fairness, she broke up with me," I tell him. "Could I convince you to put that thing down?"

He looks from it to me and back again. "Not loaded," he says finally, and clutches it tighter.

A gun's always loaded unless you've pulled the shells out of it yourself, but I'm not going to argue with him. Not while he's holding the possibly loaded gun.

"Can I talk to Hanna?"

He scowls. "She's not home."

"Please, Mr. Hott. Not sure if you ever did something stupid on your way to figuring out who you were, but I've done plenty of it. One of those stupid things was not figuring out faster exactly what my feelings for Hanna were. And then not doing everything in my power to tell her. But now I know, and I'll tell her."

The grizzled rancher in front of me gives me a long,

jaded look. "Words," he says, and spits past me so it lands on the welcome mat. "Hanna doesn't need pretty words. She needs someone to take care of her and be her family when I'm gone. And at the moment, it doesn't look like those deadbeat brothers of hers are planning to step up to the job."

"With all due respect," I say, "I don't think Hanna needs anyone to take care of her. She's one of the most capable women I've ever met. But as for being her family, I already am. I always have been. I always will be. And so will my whole family, for as long as she needs us. Hanna may be a Hott by birth, but she's a Wilder for life."

If she wants to be. If there's a human being more stubborn than the one standing in front of me, it's Hanna, and I still have to convince her to let me love her.

He gives a long, slow nod. "All right, then," he says. "You'll find her down by the river."

"Shoulda gone there first," I mutter.

"Maybe," he says. "But then we wouldn't-a had this nice chat."

"Glad you enjoyed it," I say.

I meet his eyes to discover a nearly imperceptible flash of amusement in them.

I know Fox Hott's a hard man. I know he was hard on his grandkids, hard enough that when it came time for Hanna's brothers to decide where they wanted to be in the world, Rush Creek and the Hott ranch weren't on the short list. But at the same time, he has been the one constant in Hanna's life. The one person who's always been there for her, through thick and thin.

I guess that means Fox is family, too.

I stick my hand out. He eyes it.

"You're pushing your luck," he warns.

"I'm a Wilder," I remind him. "That's what we do."

We shake.

The last thing I hear as I head for the river is him calling after me, "I'll kill you if you hurt her."

I FIND her down by the river, skipping stones.

I hunt around on the bank. I've stripped so many good skipping stones from the ground, I'm afraid one day I won't be able to find one.

But today's not that day. I press a stone into her palm. She skips it. I hand her another.

I take a deep breath.

"I'm not taking the job," I tell her. "I turned it down. I negotiated something better with Gabe. I'm staying in Rush Creek."

She turns swiftly, sharply, the way you turn right before you yell at someone, but she doesn't. She just stares at me.

"I don't have a grand gesture," I tell her. "But I have a promise. This is how it's going to be." I take a deep breath. "Every time. I will always show up. I will always be there. I will never leave. Because I love you. I think I always have."

She turns away from me, and I don't know what that means. It hurts under my ribs, but I keep going, because Gabe and Brody were right: I can't expect her to know how I feel if I don't tell her.

"I definitely already loved you the day your mom died. I didn't know it in words. It took me a long time to know it in words. Mostly I just knew I needed to be where you were. I needed to give you something to hold onto. And I needed to give you a reason to laugh. That's what I knew. But now I know all those things are love. I'm not going to stop loving you. This isn't a lark, it isn't temporary, it isn't going to end."

Her shoulders shake—she's crying, I realize, with a sudden bolt of pain.

She sinks down onto the ground, shoulders heaving.

I've never seen Hanna cry, but I feel like I know exactly what to do. I sink down next to her and gather her into my arms.

"You shouldn't turn down the job because of me."

Hanna is not a pretty crier, but I don't give a shit, because having this woman be her worst—and therefore best—self in my arms is far and away the peak, most amazing, thing that has ever happened to me.

I tell her, "Because of you is the best reason I know."

This sends her into fresh sobs.

"I'm not leaving," I say.

"You can't promise that," she says.

I know exactly what she means. She's been left all kinds of ways. Her mother couldn't promise she'd stay. My father couldn't either. There's nothing I can do to take the sting out of that. But I can hold her. So I do. Tight.

Finally, she takes a deep, shuddering breath and says, "I'm scared."

I wonder if Hanna has ever said those words before in her life. I think probably not. They're like a gift. Like a stone she pressed into my palm.

"I know," I tell her.

We're both quiet for a long time.

"How do I know you won't get tired of me? Bored? You're very pretty, and a lot of women want to lick you."

I laugh, pressing my face into her hair. The soft strands are a feather tease on my skin, and the floral scent of her twines itself around my senses. "Not nearly as many as you think."

"Even my grandfather knows you're a panty melter and warned me to stay away from you."

"Your panties are the only ones I want to melt."

"Do you understand what I'm saying, Easton? I'm saying, I'm so scared you aren't serious about this."

I'm not hurt, because I know exactly how serious I am. And how hard it is for her to trust that—or anything. "This is the thing I am most serious about in the whole entire world."

"Everyone leaves," she says. "Everyone fucking leaves."

"I know, Han."

"I kept you at a distance all these years because *that* didn't scare the shit out of me. Now you're in here"—she taps her chest—"and I just feel so utterly fucked."

The only possible answer to that is the truth. "Me too."

I pick up one more stone and press it into her hand. She draws a deep, shuddering breath.

It's the first time I feel like I can breathe, too.

She looks at me, tearstained, snotty, the most beautiful thing I've ever seen.

"I want to show you something," she says.

45

HANNA

I feel wobbly, like a colt on new legs, as we walk up from the river and around the back of the east stables —which are being rented these days by a riding school that lost its own stables to fire.

Behind the stables, there's an apple tree.

"This is the tree I planted with my mom when I was six," I tell Easton.

His eyes move from the tree to my face, curious, and—

I don't mind. I want him to see me. I want him to know me. Maybe it'll take a while before I trust him completely, but I'm going to try—if that means I get this. Easton, by my side. Easton telling me he loves me.

"It was a good day. It was a day we didn't fight about what I should wear or how girls should sit or whether I could cut all my hair off. She loved gardening, and I didn't hate it, and that was enough. So, she got this tree, and we planted it together.

"I didn't know this was here."

"I don't show anyone."

I kneel in the grass. Reach up, take his hand, tug him down. He joins me there, his warm bulk settling close in beside me, so close I can smell his forest-meets-river scent, as familiar to me as the land around me.

In the dirt under the tree are stones—smooth, round, flat. Skipping stones.

"Stones you've given me," I explain. Easton makes a small noise, a huff of breath. When I look at him, he's looking back at me, and the expression on his face—

I think it's gratitude. Like I've given him a gift.

"The ones you put in your pocket," he murmurs, touching the stones, one after another.

"There's always one in my pocket." I laugh. "Well. At least when I was wearing hiking pants. Leggings, not so much. Although the new leggings—" I grin at him. "They have a pocket in the back, right over my butt. So sometimes I carry one there.

"Anyway, whenever you give me a new one, I take the old one out of my pocket and put it here."

I point. "This is the one I put in my pocket the day my mom died." I show him, and he strokes his fingertip over it. I feel that touch, feather light.

"This one's from the day Gabe phased out skiing, and this one's from the day Mack Galt asked me to co-star in his porn flicks, and this one's from—"

"The day you came back from that date with Nan's nephew, the one where he took you geocaching, and she fed him lines. I recognize it. It was stripey."

"This is the one I put in my pocket on the first Bear trip, when he was flirting with that redhead and you said, 'Good thing you don't have a crush on him.'"

His eyes are steady on my face. Green, bright, full of love.

I look down at the stones and then up at Easton. "I didn't understand why I was saving them. But now I do. It was because they were my ballast. They were the steadiest, most dependable thing in my life. And I liked being able to look at them and know you were there. I *loved* being able to look at them and know you were there."

The way he's looking at me, I feel a little unhinged. Unmoored. But it's okay. I reach out a hand, and he takes it, and it connects me back to myself.

"I love you," I whisper.

It's barely loud enough for me to hear, which means it's barely loud enough for him to hear, but he clutches my hand tighter, so I know he did.

"I love you, too," he says. Right out loud, so the tree and the stones can hear. "Also, I really want to—"

He doesn't finish the sentence. Instead, he kisses me.

The grass is soft as we sink down together.

As my back meets the ground, he says, "It's a really good thing you didn't have a crush on Bear Warden." His hand slips behind my head, stroking my hair. "Because that guy didn't stand a chance."

"No," I say, as his thigh presses between mine. "He didn't."

46

HANNA

It turns out that even if you are an inveterate panty melter, you probably do not actually carry condoms everywhere you go. So Easton and I go back to his place, where we stay for two nights and three days, ordering takeout, finishing his whole Ben & Jerrys and popcorn stash, bingeing *Bridgerton*, and...

Mmm.

Lots and lots of that.

Late on the third day, I get a text from my girlfriends. They're having an impromptu girls' night out, and they want me to join them at Rachel's, where we will be watching the K-Drama *It's Okay to Not Be Okay*, eating peanut butter M&Ms and pretzels, and divvying up some sex toy overstock that Rachel says will cost her more to try to sell or return than is worth her time.

"I don't know," I say, putting my phone down.

"Why wouldn't you go?"

"Because it might just be an excuse to try to get information out of me. About you. How I *feel* about you."

"Would that be so bad?" he asks, eyebrow raised. "You told *me* how you feel about me, and the world kept spinning."

"But they're—?"

"They're what?" he wants to know. "They're your friends. And I know you don't want to believe this, for some reason that is totally foreign to me, but they *love* you. They want you to be happy. And they want to share in your happiness. Besides," he says, mock grumpily, "I'm starting to feel left out because I'm the only Wilder brother who's never been the subject of the whole girl squad of gossip."

"This is actually about how you want me to claim you in front of them."

"Yeah, basically," he says.

I hesitate, still.

"You can come back here afterwards, and we can have sex in the shower again. *And I'll use the shower head on you.*"

"Oh. Well, then," I tease him. "That's all the incentive I'll ever need to do your bidding."

In the end, I go.

They're all there. Amanda, Lucy, Rachel, Jessa, Imani, Mari. When I knock on the door, Rachel answers and ushers me in. Everyone greets me, and I seat myself on the floor because that's the best access to the peanut butter M&Ms and popcorn.

Then they go right back to what they were talking about, which is pregnancy cravings. I guess Mari has a thing for Boston cream pie and Amanda ate nothing but grapefruit and for Lucy it was all about this one kind of British tea cookies.

After a while, I get weirdly impatient, and before I can

stop myself, I blurt, "Aren't you going to ask me about Easton?"

All six of them turn to stare at me.

Amanda opens her mouth, but Lucy speaks first. "No," she says. "We weren't going to ask. Because we didn't think you wanted to talk about it." Her voice and her eyes are soft as she says it. "We didn't want to make you uncomfortable. You hate it when we ask you stuff about yourself."

I think about how it feels to be just a little bit on the outside. Not quite a Hott brother. Not quite a Wilder. Not quite one of the boys, not quite one of the girls. It's a feeling I'm used to. I don't like the feeling, but I don't hate it, either. It's, oddly enough, a *safe* feeling.

Showing Easton the stones, that wasn't safe.

Telling Easton I love him, that wasn't safe.

Letting myself want Easton to stay here and love me for, possibly forever? Not safe at all.

And yet, after the leap, after the terrifying, heart-stopping, falling-like-I've-just-stepped-out-of-an-airplane...

It's different from how I thought it would be.

Better.

Richer.

Sweeter.

And these last three days with Easton? I've felt *safer*, too.

Which makes no sense. How is it possible that something so dangerous could make me feel like I'm wrapped in a warm blanket?

They're all still watching me quietly, but Amanda starts to shift, and I can tell from her body language that she's about to open a new topic of conversation, take the focus off me, so I blurt:

"It's not that I don't *want* to talk about myself or my feelings. It's that I don't know *how* to. I don't have any practice."

"Well," says Amanda, pragmatic as ever. "You're not going to get any better at it if you don't try, right?"

"Right," I say.

"We'll break you in slowly. None of that, 'So? Are you in love with him?!!!' stuff that we foisted on Lucy and Rachel," Amanda says decisively. "We'll start with easy questions, like *how the* hell *did this happen*?"

Everyone laughs, including me.

I open my mouth to start. "It started when Bear came to town and I decided I had a crush on him."

But as the words are coming out of my mouth, I realize: Sure, they're the truth, but they're not really *my* truth.

"Wait. Is it okay if I go a little further back in time?"

They all nod at me.

"My mom and I—we didn't really see eye to eye on a lot of stuff. But when she died, I—"

My voice breaks. Actually, everything kind of breaks right then. My voice, the wall holding back my grief, the levy holding back my tears. It turns out that once you cry, it's easier to cry even more. Not sure how I feel about that... but here we are.

Amanda hands me a box of tissues. She does that all the time, but this is the first time it's been me. Me clutching the tissues, me with the tears rolling down my face, me struggling to catch my breath and pick up the thread of the story.

"Don't rush," Lucy says.

"We have all night," Jessa says.

"And if you change your mind and don't want to tell us, you don't have to," Mari says.

"But if you want to tell us, we don't care how neat and pretty it is," Imani says.

"We just want to know you better," Rachel says.

And for the first time ever, I believe them.

EPILOGUE
EASTON

"Dance with me?"

"Do I look like I dance?" Hanna demands.

"Yup," I tell her, and spin her out onto the dance floor.

We're in a tent on the Hott property, and it's Hanna's granddad's eighty-fifth birthday party.

Hanna is, true to her own self-assessment, not notably graceful, but I don't give a crap. I just want her in my arms.

And I want to distract her from her sadness at the fact that her brothers aren't here.

She tracked down the brother who'd gone off the grid and pleaded with all of them in email. And to be fair, their replies were kind. They all said they wanted to see her, that they missed her, that they were sorry things had worked out the way they had.

And they all said they couldn't leave behind their busy lives to celebrate a man who, at best, had been a block of wood.

She resigned herself to that reality, but she's a little melancholy tonight, so I've gone out of my way to cheer her up any way I can. Mostly that has involved bringing her sparkly drinks and plates of food, and forcing her to hit the piñata with me.

And most recently, coercing her into dancing.

Most of the women here are wearing short gowns, but Hanna is wearing this raspberry-colored sexy cropped halter-top-and-shorts combo that's way sexier than any of the boring little-black-dresses that surround her. After discovering her bad, hot self, Hanna has fully embraced tighter and more revealing clothes, and I am completely here for it. Right now, for example, my hands are all over her mostly bare back. Her arms and shoulders are all silky, exposed skin. And the flower-scent of her wafts up and fills my brain, making me—

Well, making me hold her a little too close. I mean, not too close for my purposes… and not too close for hers (she wiggles naughtily against me)… but this is a family party, so when I start getting hard under my not-very-forgiving suit pants, I back the hell off and spin her away from me.

All around us people are having a blast. There may not be a lot of Hotts in attendance, but that's more than made up for by the number of Wilders who are here, supporting Hanna and letting her know she's surrounded by family and friends.

"Good thing it stayed warm," Hanna says, smashing into my chest, rocking me back on my heels, and clutching my arm for balance. I stop us both from going down, while making sure to properly enjoy the feel of her body against mine. "Because I couldn't wear a bra with this thing, and it would have been awful nipply. Not to mention all the goosebumps."

"Nipply's a bad thing?" I murmur, brushing my lips across her ear. Which causes a fine layer of gooseflesh to rise all over the bare parts of Hanna that I'm currently enjoying. I sigh. The party is starting to feel long, especially because I promised Hanna yet another shower afterwards. The term "giving head" has a very special meaning in our house, aka my apartment, where we now live together.

It's summer now, and Bear and Cypress have gone back to Colorado. Hanna and I have stayed in touch with them—I think that despite everything that happened, you could say we're all friends. They'll be back this fall for a one-time special mushroom-gathering workshop.

After they left, Hanna and I hosted a foraging trip together. We fought about pretty much everything—where to go, how much gear to pack, the definition of "foraging"—but it was a huge success by every measure. Apparently—just like Lucy predicted—we're our very own comedy show, as we discovered when we started putting videos we made together up on YouTube and TikTok. The videos have been wildly successful, and Lucy has all kinds of charts to show how many new signups have come in because of them. Gabe told me yesterday that Wilder is on track to make all of us very financially comfortable over the next several years. When I told that to Hanna she said, very dryly, that that would keep me in designer shirts for decades to come... and then she admitted that she *likes* the shirts, and then she removed the one I was wearing.

The lights dim and Hanna's aunt Meryl appears at the edge of the tent with a huge birthday cake absolutely covered with candles. Hanna and I are standing right next to Hanna's granddad as the partygoers launch into "Happy

Birthday" in the usual combination of twenty different keys. If I'm not completely mistaken, Fox Hott positively glows with pleasure. I mean, he's not *smiling* or anything, but he looks... well, not miserable.

"Don't you dare help me blow out the candles," he warns his granddaughter—vintage Fox—and then manages to do it himself with one huge breath. Pretty impressive for eighty-five.

"What'd you wish for?" Hanna asks him, as various Wilder women crowd around to help Meryl cut and serve pieces of cake.

Fox glowers. "I wished your brothers would get their heads out of their asses."

"Literally?" Hanna asks.

"Exactly those words." Fox crosses his arms.

"Well? Maybe they will," Hanna says doubtfully.

"Maybe," Fox says, his bushy gray eyebrows ticking up a notch. "But I'm not going to count on it. I have a plan. You and I, we're going to remake this property into your legacy, and they're going to help."

Startled, Hanna says, "They're going to help?"

"Yep," Fox says, with satisfaction. "Whether they like it or not. I'm going to win this in the end."

And then he takes the first piece of cake, shoves it in his mouth, and tromps away.

"Wow," I say. "What do you think he means by that?"

"I don't know," Hanna says, laughing, "but I'm guessing it's not good for my brothers."

"Probably not," I agree.

"My grandfather's pretty stubborn, and I wouldn't bet against him."

We both stare at Fox as he does the grumpy rancher version of schmoozing with his birthday guests.

"I mean, how much trouble can he cause?"

She bites her lip. "Guess we'll find out?"

"Well," I say. "Whatever happens next, I'm here. And I'm not going anywhere."

"I mean, you kind of are," she says, raising an eyebrow, mischief rolling onto her face. She grins at me. "Home with me, stat. But first, you're going to grab us two pieces of that cake, to go."

ACKNOWLEDGMENTS

I'm having a bit of a moment here.

At the end of 2020, in cahoots with author buddies Dylann Crush and Megan Ryder (to whom I am eternally grateful), I dreamed up the Wilders. They became my playmates and favorite imaginary friends for the next two years. And now this series is done, and I have to say goodbye.

It's hard! I love these characters. And I have loved watching you, dear readers, love these characters. The Wilders are special to me, but most of all because they have made you laugh and cry and write me emails and beg for more. And I have loved every minute of it.

But there is good news, too! As you may have guessed from how we left Hanna at the end of this book, you have not seen the last of her—or Easton, his brothers, and their wives, girlfriends, and kiddos. My next series will feature a whole new family, the Hotts, but a familiar environment— Rush Creek—and many of the characters and secondary characters you have come to love.

I hope you will laugh and cry and write me emails and beg for more of them, too, because that's why I do this!

One particular reader gets her name in lights this time around. Congratulations and thank you to Tilly Henderson, aka @bookishspoonie on Instagram, who won a contest in my reader group and named Britney, Hanna's nemesis. I warned Tilly that Britney might not make it all the way to publication—and her role in the book did get a bit diminished from how I'd originally imagined it—but she stuck it out and made it onto the final pages. Tilly, thank you for playing, and I hope you enjoy seeing Britney's name in print—and yours!

Thank you so much to my early readers, Dylann Crush, Rachel Grant, Christina Hovland, and Brenda St. John Brown. Thank you for taking time away from your own stories to help make this book the best it could be. Special thanks to Donna Barker, Cathryn Fox, and Elizabeth Safleur, for being my "cold" readers—the ones who tell me whether someone entering the series with this book can make sense of the Wilder muddle.

Huge thanks also to the author friends who support me on a regular basis—Audrey, Cheryl, Dylann, Megan, Christy, Brenda, Christine, Gwen, Rachel, Kate, Kris, Karen, Susannah, Claire, Sylvie, Arell, Hope, and many, many more, including but not limited to the authors of the Corner of Smart and Sexy, RAM Rom Com, the post-RAM Brain Dump, Wide for the Win, Awesome Babes for Good Things, and my ongoing newsletter swaps.

Thank you to my agent, Emily Sylvan Kim, and my sub rights agent, Tina Shen!

Thank you, Sarah Sarai! You have been on this wild, Wilder, wildest journey, too, and it has been a delight to have you at my side for the ride. I have deeply appreciated your attention to detail and willingness to Bear (see what I did there?) with my foibles.

Thank you, XPresso Book Tours, especially Giselle, for the release blitz!

Hugs and kisses for my not-author friends who support my imaginary worlds with so much love and patience: Aimee, Chelsea, Darya, Ellen, Elizabeth, Jenn, Jess, Julia, Kathy, Lauren, Molly, Soomie, and Tracey.

To BellGirl, BellBoy, and Mr. Bell, you are the family that taught me what it feels like to belong, and what it means to find the people who make you feel like you. The Wilders and their wider world owe so much to your love and support. Mr. Bell: Every romance hero is a little bit of you, but none is as real or as kind or as steadfast. I love you all!

Any errors of fact or insensitivity relating to representation are mine and mine alone. If you note any, please let me know so I can apologize and learn to be better.

ALSO BY SERENA BELL

Wilder Adventures

Make Me Wilder

Walk on the Wilder Side

Wilder With You

A Little Wilder

Wilder at Last

Hott Springs Eternal

Hott Shot

Under One Roof

Do Over

Head Over Heels

Sleepover

Returning Home

Hold On Tight

Can't Hold Back

To Have and to Hold

Holding Out

Tierney Bay

So Close

So True

So Good (2022)

So Right (2023)

New York Glitz

Still So Hot!

Hot & Bothered

Standalone

Turn Up the Heat

ABOUT THE AUTHOR

USA Today bestselling author Serena Bell writes contemporary romance with heat, heart, and humor. A former journalist, Serena has always believed that everyone has an amazing story to tell if you listen carefully, and you can often find her scribbling in her tiny garret office, mainlining chocolate and bringing to life the tales in her head.

Serena's books have earned many honors, including a RITA finalist spot, an RT Reviewers' Choice Award, Apple Books Best Book of the Month, and Amazon Best Book of the Year for Romance.

When not writing, Serena loves to spend time with her college-sweetheart husband and two hilarious kiddos—all of whom are incredibly tolerant not just of Serena's imaginary friends but also of how often she changes her hobbies and how passionately she embraces the new ones. These days, it's stand-up paddle boarding, board-gaming, meditation, and long walks with good friends.